MURDER'S LAST RESORT

Rooftop Garden Cozy Mysteries, Book 20

THEA CAMBERT

Summer Prescott Books Publishing

Copyright 2022 Summer Prescott Books

All Rights Reserved. No part of this publication nor any of the information herein may be quoted from, nor reproduced, in any form, including but not limited to: printing, scanning, photocopying, or any other printed, digital, or audio formats, without prior express written consent of the copyright holder.

**This book is a work of fiction. Any similarities to persons, living or dead, places of business, or situations past or present, is completely unintentional.

CHAPTER 1

Alice Maguire-Evans was tired. *Really. Tired.* The problem was, she didn't have time to *be* tired.

First and foremost, a six-month-old baby, through no fault of their own, doesn't really care whether you got enough sleep last night or not. Add to that a thriving business to manage and then mix in the start of the holiday season—and what else could you expect but to be worn out?

"We set the bar too high with that Halloween party last night," said Owen James, Alice's best friend, as he plopped down into the chair next to hers. Evening was coming on, and the two were sitting above Main Street in the rooftop garden they had created along with their other best friend, Franny Brown-Maguire.

"Too high?" asked Alice, yawning.

"It was too perfect. Too much fun. We'll never be able to top it." Owen yawned, too. "What happens next year?"

"Something tells me we'll come up with something equally fabulous next year," Alice assured him.

"I mean, the food was exactly on point," Owen continued. "The kids were adorable. The games were a blast, and the costumes—don't even get me started about the costumes."

He was right about that. Alice's six-month old daughter, Isabelle—Izzy for short—had been dressed as a tiny, adorable snowy owl. Franny's toddler, Theodore—Theo for short—had helped to choose his own costume this year, and had insisted on being a chef-dragon, which was basically a dragon wearing a chef's hat. Even Owen's tiny Yorkie Franklin had come to the party decked out as a cupcake, complete with a dollop of frosting—plus sprinkles—on his head.

Franny came out into the garden, carrying a carafe and three mugs from her business downstairs, Joe's coffee shop. She set them on the table. "I made the coffee, but I'm too tired to pour it."

"Allow me," said Owen, pouring three mugs.

"And please tell me you threw in some extra caffeine."

"Trust me. Once this hits bottom, you're going to have a burst of energy," said Franny, taking a sip from her mug.

It was a chilly evening, the first of November, and the three friends had all just come off a long day of work at their respective businesses. Their building was located smack in the middle of Main Street, which was right in the center of town.

Blue Valley, Tennessee, which was still bustling even though the sun was setting, had sprung up many years ago in a picturesque valley deep in Tennessee's Smoky Mountains. The town was small enough that everyone pretty much knew everyone else, but the population swelled around weekends, holidays, and festival days. It was Wednesday evening, so the weekend tourists hadn't arrived yet, but the Halloween tourists and autumn leaf peepers were still about.

The rooftop garden was the ideal place to unwind at the end of a long day. It was also the perfect place to start your day with your morning paper and first cup of coffee. Normally, the three friends would be chatting over glasses of wine or snacks or dinner, along with their families, by the time dusk settled over the town, but they'd all agreed that today, they'd need evening coffee just to be energized enough to make dinner and stay awake until bedtime.

The garden had bloomed atop a beautiful historic building that Alice's grandmother owned. The first floor housed three shops: Owen's bakery, Sourdough, was on one end. Franny's coffee shop, Joe's was on the other. And Alice's bookstore, the Paper Owl, was right in the middle. On the second floor were three small apartments that the friends had moved into as they'd opened up shop down below—with Alice being the first to arrive. That first day—it was eleven years ago now—when Alice, then just out of college, had explored the building, she felt she'd found the perfect spot to pursue her dream of owning her own bookstore. She'd moved her meager belongings into the apartment above the shop, and when she'd walked through the double French doors that led from her living room out onto the rooftop, she'd had a vision. Sure, it was just a desolate space at the time. But Alice imagined a small vegetable garden, pots of fresh herbs and flowers, archways covered in vines, and twinkling lights everywhere.

Franny, who had been Alice's best friend since middle school, opened her coffee shop and loved the idea. And finally, Owen, who had moved to Blue

Valley at age twenty-nine to open Sourdough, had filled out the third apartment and had brought along his own creative ideas for the garden. The three of them together had created a whimsical haven above Main Street—and that was just the beginning.

Soon, other businesses up and down the street got inspired and followed suit. The Smiling Hound pub just across the street and up a few doors, created an outdoor seating area for customers on their rooftop, complete with lights and trailing vines that spilled over the building's front façade. Directly across the street, there was a sort of Zen garden where Koi Butler, who owned the yoga studio below, could be spotted doing sun salutations and enjoying early morning matcha as the sun rose each day. There were also gardens, twinkling lights, and outdoor sitting areas above Blue Beauty Spa, Crumpets, and Sugar Buzz, among others. These days, when newcomers arrived in town, they were usually both surprised and delighted when in the middle of strolling down Main Street, they happened to look upward.

"Let's really rest this weekend," Franny suggested. "Seriously. Let's just promise ourselves that we'll take walks and read and sleep whenever possible, all weekend long."

"And eat takeout," added Owen. "No cooking."

"We're heading out to the lake tomorrow," Alice reminded them.

As their families had expanded, all three of the friends had acquired small homes on Blue Lake, about a mile from the center of town. Alice's brother Ben, who was now chief of the local police force, had been the first to move there. He'd loved growing up hanging out at the lake, so when a small house at the east end had come on the market, he'd jumped on it. Then he'd fallen head over heels in love with Franny, who was already settled into her apartment above Joe's. But Franny loved Ben's house at the lake just as much as she loved her Main Street apartment, so they split their time between the two.

When the police department had finally gotten around to hiring a detective, Luke Evans had moved to town and had purchased and renovated the cozy cabin next door to Ben's house. Subsequently, Alice and Luke had fallen in love and gotten married so that the cabin became Alice's home too.

Just around the lake's bend from Alice and Luke's house had been an old, historic cottage that was falling apart. Owen had surprised everyone when he'd bought it and restored it beyond its former glory. Owen had married Michael Boyd, who was the head concierge at the local mountain resort as well as being a brilliant and respected poet.

Now, with their families expanded to include children as well as pets, the group of friends tended to stay in town at their apartments when there were festivals or the like going on and business was hopping. It was handy to be able to just walk downstairs to go to work or to duck upstairs to put the children down for their naps. The rest of the time, they were all neighbors at the lake—and Alice was most definitely looking forward to spending the holiday season at her and Luke's cabin. She would put swags of fall leaves on the porch railings and string extra lights around the dock, sit outside reading and looking over the glistening water, and curl up by the stone fireplace come evening.

She yawned again just thinking about it. "The fall festival starts next week. There's so much to do to get ready. And then Thanksgiving will be here before you know it. And then we have the Hometown Holiday Festival after that."

"Christmas tree hunting. Decorating . . ." Owen added.

"Shopping for gifts. Cooking and baking and holiday cards . . ." said Franny.

"I love every bit of that stuff," said Alice. "But

you're right. We really do need a break." She set down her coffee mug and turned in her chair to face the others. "Let's make a deal. We're all off from work this weekend. Beginning Friday night, we all just unwind and have a guilt-free lazy weekend."

"Agreed," said Owen, raising his mug.

Just then, Alice's cat, Poppy, who had been snoozing under the table, hopped up, fully alert.

"The Poppy alarm," said Franny. "That means the guys are coming up the stairs."

Down on the first floor, there was a long hallway that ran the length of the back of the building. It housed the three doors that led into the backs of the shops, as well as the main back door that led into a small parking lot. The hallway also held a beautiful old wooden staircase that led up to the apartments on the second floor.

Poppy, a small mild-mannered calico, adored Alice's brother Ben, and always knew when he had entered the building. As soon as he emerged through the French doors in Alice's apartment and came out into the garden with Luke right behind him, Poppy ran over and wound around his legs. She then honored Luke with similar treatment. The two men came and took their usual seats in the circle of

Adirondack chairs, Poppy hopping into Luke's lap and demanding his full attention.

"It's chilly out here," said Ben. "I'll build us a fire."

Owen had added a fire ring to the garden some time ago, and it was perfect for fall evenings when they all wanted to stay outside. Just then, Alice could hear Izzy moving around in her crib through the baby monitor. She got up and Luke gently set Poppy down and followed his wife into the apartment.

"You'll never guess what happened to Ben and me just now," he said, getting out a fresh diaper for their daughter.

"You're probably right about that," said Alice. "I'm too tired to guess."

"We both got the weekend off, starting tomorrow."

"A long weekend? That *never* happens!" Alice scooped up Izzy and brought her to the changing table. "We were just saying that we all could use a break before the holidays get into full swing."

"And with the fall festival starting next week, things are about to get busy. Here, let me do it. You sit."

Alice gladly accepted his offer and sat in the

rocking chair while Luke changed Izzy's diaper. "I can't wait to get out to the cabin and just relax. Owen and Franny and I all agreed to be lazy bums all weekend."

"That's the best plan I've heard all year," said Luke, finishing up with Izzy's diaper and picking her up. "Let's go whip up some dinner and eat outside by the fire."

When they returned to the garden, a nice fire was crackling away in the fire ring, and Michael had arrived home bearing two large, hot, cheesy pizzas from Pie in the Sky down the street.

"I thought everyone could use a night off after last night's party," he said, passing out plates.

"You are the best," said Franny, who had just set Theo up in his highchair with a few crackers and small blocks of cheese, which he seemed to be enjoying immensely. He was still wrapped up in the thrill of being able to feed himself and was all about any kind of food he could pick up with his dimpled fingers.

"That's why I married him," sang Owen, taking a slice of sausage and cheese and setting it on his plate.

"I wanted to celebrate," said Michael. "I actually got the weekend off!"

"You're kidding! So did we!" said Ben.

"The stars must be aligning," said Alice. "We're all off!"

"Staycation!" said Franny. "Let's go out to the lake and do absolutely nothing."

"All I have to do is put in the fall garden," said Ben. "But that'll be fun."

"And I have to repair that loose railing on our porch," added Luke. "No big deal."

"The laundry isn't going to do itself, of course . . ." Franny admitted. "But it won't take much time or energy."

Theo clapped his hands and called for more cheese, so Ben ran into the apartment. Izzy began to fuss, so Alice hurried to mix up her bowl of rice cereal with pureed bananas.

"I guess you can't really be too lazy when you're a parent," she said, finally sitting down with a slice of pizza. She inhaled deeply the scents of sausage and cheese, woodsmoke and fallen leaves. "But we'll do our best."

CHAPTER 2

It was midmorning the next day when Henry Witherspoon, Blue Valley's downtown postal carrier, dropped off Alice's mail. Alice had climbed up into the front window of the Paper Owl, where she was busy creating a Thanksgiving display that involved a giant turkey whose colorful tail feathers each featured a different book with a fall setting. Swagged above that was a banner made of autumn-colored flags that read, *Thankful for good books*. The turkey, in one feathered hand, was holding a sign that said *Come gobble up your next great read today!*

Henry examined the display from outside, then came in, jingling the bells over the front door. "That's pretty clever, Alice," he said with a laugh. "Want me to leave your mail on the counter?"

"Thanks, Henry. Just give it to Hazel."

Henry gave a little salute, stopped to say hello to Izzy, who was having a grand time in her bouncy seat as her mother worked, then carried the small stack of magazines, catalogues, and letters over to Hazel Smithers, Alice's assistant at the shop. Alice saw Henry digging through his bag for Franny's mail as he walked through the large cased opening that separated the Paper Owl from Joe's.

A moment later, Hazel wandered over to the front window. "Need any help there, Alice?"

Alice stood, bumping her head on the ceiling of the window display compartment. "Ouch!" She climbed down to stand next to Hazel. "Let's go see how it looks," she said, lifting Izzy out of her seat and leading the way out to the sidewalk in front of the shop.

When both women had agreed that the display was equal parts whimsical and informative, they came back inside.

"Oh—I wanted to show you something. Look at this, Alice," said Hazel. "It was in today's mail. Looks fancy."

"It certainly does," said Alice, securing Izzy back in her bouncy seat and taking the oversized, crisp white envelope from Hazel's hand. "Probably some kind of advertisement." She turned the envelope over and slid a finger under the flap, then pulled out a beautifully engraved invitation. As she read the words, her eyes grew wider and wider.

"What is it?" asked Hazel, trying to read upside down.

"It's an invitation to a pre-opening weekend at a new resort called The Abbey." Alice read the small card that had been inside the envelope as well. "These are the directions to get there . . . Oh—it's just outside of town, up in the mountains." She turned the envelope over, glancing at the return address, then looked inside the envelope to see if there was anything else there. It was empty. "This must be some kind of marketing scheme." She handed the invitation back to Hazel and picked up Izzy's seat by the handle.

"It says here it's all expenses paid!" said Hazel, trotting along behind Alice as she went back over to the counter. "You should go!"

"Hazel," said Alice, "when you've been in business as long as I have, you learn that people will do all kinds of things to get you to buy whatever it is they're selling. I'm sure there's some hidden fee or catch."

"Hey, look what I got!" Franny came running over

from Joe's, Theo on her hip, waving a large white envelope.

"Let me guess," said Alice. "An invitation to a mountain resort."

"How did—" Franny looked at the invitation in Hazel's hands. "You got one too?"

"Franny, there's no way this is a legitimate invitation. I bet everybody in town got one," said Alice.

The shop's backdoor, which looked like just another bookshelf, flew open and Owen came running in.

"Owen! What if a customer had been looking at the books there?" said Alice. "I've told you to open that door *slowly*."

"Sorry," said Owen, looking back to check that he hadn't pummeled anyone with the door. "I was so excited I forgot. Look what came in the mail today!"

Franny's shoulders sagged. "So I guess you're right, Alice. Everyone in town must've gotten one." She set Theo down and he toddled straight over to his Uncle Owen.

"Gotten one what?" asked Owen, picking Theo up. "Surely you don't mean this." He shifted Theo to one arm and held up his large white envelope.

"Yep," said Franny. "We both got one too. Alice thinks it's a marketing ploy or something."

Owen gave Theo a peck on the head, set him down, and slipped his invitation out of the envelope and held it to the light. He ran his fingers over the words. "I don't think so. This thing is engraved. And it's printed on superfine cardstock with an eggshell finish." He turned the envelope over and pointed at it. "This is a real stamp—not a bulk mailing label. *And* it's an oversized envelope. That means extra postage. Do you have any idea what it would cost to mail these things out to everyone in town?"

Alice peered at Owen's envelope. "It's addressed to both you and Michael." She picked up her own envelope. "And mine is addressed to Mr. and Mrs. Luke Evans."

"Ben's invited too," said Franny, holding up hers.

Alice frowned. She pulled out the invitation and examined it again. "It just says, *you're cordially invited*. It doesn't say *you'll have a chance to invest* or *you're getting a big discount* . . ."

"Nope," said Franny, excited hope returning to her eyes. "It says all-inclusive, all expenses paid."

"It also says it starts today," said Owen, pointing to that detail.

"Are you serious? *Today*?" asked Alice. "This is very strange."

"Stay here," said Owen, heading for the front door

and pulling it open. "I'm going to do a little research." He disappeared from view as he scuttled down the sidewalk.

Alice and Hazel got back to work in the bookshop and Franny took Theo and went back into Joe's, joining her assistant manager, Beth, behind the counter. About a quarter of an hour later, Owen threw open the front door and entered the bookshop, a triumphant look on his face.

"You can put away your skepticism, Alice, my friend, because no one else on Main Street got one of these babies." He waved his invitation in the air. "We're the only ones."

Franny came running in. "Did you say we're the only ones?"

"Yep," said Owen. "And Pearl Ann says she's heard about this place."

That was no surprise. Pearl Ann McKenzie had her finger on the pulse of the entire valley. She knew everything about everyone *and* their uncle.

"What did she say about it?" asked Franny.

"That it's supposed to be seriously swanky," said Owen. He cleared his throat. "And cursed."

"Swanky?" said Franny, wiggling her eyebrows.

"Cursed?" said Alice, putting her hands on her hips.

Owen nodded. "Apparently back in the mid-1800s it was a monastery. A little band of French Trappist monks lived there. That's why it's call The Abbey."

"French Trappist monks? In Tennessee?" asked Alice.

Owen held up his hands. "That's what Pearl Ann said. And there's a story that something happened up there—a fire or something? Pearl Ann didn't have the details. Anyway, it had been deserted for a long time. It's really remote. And then this wealthy guy bought it and transformed it into a luxury resort with a spa and everything! The grand opening is supposed to be next week."

"So he's inviting us for a *pre*-grand opening?" said Alice.

Franny sighed, glancing through the cased opening where Beth had been joined by Officer Dewey, a colleague of Ben and Luke's. Dewey was flying Theo around the room, making airplane noises and Theo was giggling his heart out. "It doesn't really sound like the ideal place to take children. And we'd have to drive up there today. That's not a lot of advanced notice."

The bells above the door jingled and Bea Maguire, Alice and Ben's mother, breezed in. "I'm here for my grandchildren," she said, walking over to join them.

The Maguires still lived in the cozy house Alice and Ben had grown up in, about half a block away across the street from Town Park. They, along with Franny's parents, were the children's foremost babysitters, although both kids spent a morning or two a week at Little Sprouts, the daycare center around the corner from the bookshop. Franny's parents lived a short walk away as well, on Azalea Street right next door to Alice and Ben's granny. Sometimes the grandparents were so available and ready to help out with the kids that Alice and Franny found themselves having to stave them off a bit. But mostly, they were just grateful that the children were so loved and well taken care of—especially on busy days on Main Street.

Bea made a beeline for her granddaughter, who was still exuberantly kicking her little feet to make her chair bounce wildly. "And how is my little Isabelle Beatrice doing today?"

Izzy returned her biggest smile.

"Is that a tiny tooth I see?" said Bea, leaning in closer. "Oh Alice, we need to get out the teething ring your father and I bought and put in a supply of those teething biscuits."

Alice had noticed the first bottom baby tooth poking through just that morning. "I'll pick some up when I run out for groceries after work."

"I hear from Ben that you all have the weekend off," said Bea, unbuckling Izzy and lifting her out of her seat. "How nice! I bet you'll be getting a start on your fall cleaning ahead of the holidays! The festival is next week, after all, and things stay pretty busy after that all the way through New Year's Day."

Alice nodded slowly, suddenly feeling tired again.

"Or . . ." Franny said, picking up Alice's invitation, "We might do this this weekend. We're all invited."

Bea took the invitation and read it. Her face lit up. "I've heard about this place. Sounds like it's going to be five-star all the way." She looked from Alice to Franny. "We'd be happy to keep the kids if you want to go." She gave Owen a smile. "And the pets, too."

Alice felt the weight on her shoulders suddenly easing up. "You would? Are you sure? The invitation says to come today."

"Of course I'm sure," said Bea without hesitation. "I mean, how often do you get the opportunity to attend something like this? If you like the place, your father and I will have to go up the mountain for our anniversary!" She frowned. "I wonder how the owner chose the guests . . . I bet they're hoping you three will talk the place up in your shops—put the word out."

"That makes sense," said Alice. She looked at Owen and Franny. "And I guess if we get up there and it turns out to be a ruse, we can always just come back down."

"True," said Franny. "Bea, are you sure you want both kids all weekend? You know my parents will be glad to take turns."

"I know they will, and I promise we'll call them and let them have some time with the grandkids too. You three and your spouses should just go relax and recharge! How lovely!"

"I'm calling Ben," said Franny, giving her mother-in-law a hug. "We need to pack!"

"I'll call Michael and you get in touch with Luke," said Owen, heading for the back door.

Bea smiled at Alice. "My dear, sometimes opportunity knocks. And if you hesitate, it might not wait around outside the door, you know. Go. Have a fun weekend. Take a *vacation*, for goodness' sake. The kids will be safe and sound at our house."

Alice smiled. "No laundry? Or fall cleaning? Or gardening? Just a whole weekend of reading and sleeping and eating . . . How could I refuse?"

CHAPTER 3

The road up to The Abbey was a winding one, indeed. Everyone piled into Owen and Michael's SUV and they started their journey after dropping Izzy and Theo, along with Franklin, Finn, and Poppy, at the Maguires' house. Alice felt a pang of separation anxiety from her little one, but it helped to snuggle up to Luke in the backseat. Franny and Ben were in the third row of seats behind them, and Owen was at the wheel with Michael calling out the directions from the card they'd received with their invitations.

"Are we there yet?" asked Franny. "This road is twistier than a snake."

"But the views are breathtaking," said Alice, looking out over the valley from her window. The whole town below them looked like a collection of toys, the sun glinting momentarily off the surface of Blue Lake but then fading as the clouds drifted in.

"Looks like rain," said Luke, leaning to peer up at the sky.

"Perfect!" said Alice, snuggling closer to him. "What could be cozier than a rainy weekend at a secluded retreat?"

"The entrance should be just around this next bend," said Michael. "Yep. There it is."

If the entrance was any indication, they were in for a lovely weekend. The gate stood open in the wooden fence, which was fully landscaped with roses climbing up it and garden beds all along it. On either side of the entry road was a square stone column that looked as old as the mountains but that had been scrupulously maintained. On the left column was a simple brass plaque with the words *The Retreat* engraved in crisp letters in its surface.

"No giant welcome signs or flags flapping the breeze," Michael observed. "Just understated elegance."

They proceeded down the long drive, which passed between clusters of trees and several small orchards, before coming to a large wood and stone building that boasted huge windows which shone spotless in the afternoon light.

"I feel underdressed," said Alice, looking down at her simple cardigan, t-shirt, and jeans.

"Well, you look beautiful," said Luke, leaning over to kiss her.

They all lumbered out of the car and into the huge double doors of the building. They emerged into a welcoming room, its ceiling two stories high at least. There were chairs and couches arranged in clusters near a massive fireplace with logs crackling and sputtering inside, giving off the glorious scent of pine. To the right was a long, gleaming wooden counter with a smiling, uniformed woman standing behind it.

"Hello and welcome to The Abbey," she said as they approached. "You are Alice and Luke Evans, Franny and Ben Maguire, Owen James, and Michael Boyd." She gave Michael a wink. "I hear you're in the resort business too, sir."

"I am," said Michael, surprised.

"I am Mrs. Bentley. Once The Abbey opens, I'll be head of housekeeping here, but this weekend, we have only opened to a very few choice guests, so we're down to a minimal staff. Your host will explain everything. Meanwhile, here are your keys. Your cottages are in cluster three, which you can see on this map." She handed Owen a map with their cottages highlighted. "Please feel free to go and get settled in."

They thanked Mrs. Bentley and headed back to the car, following the map of the property. They pulled around behind the large building to find a green scattered with trees, with winding stone pathways crisscrossing it, leading to the different structures that stood there—many of them the clusters of small stone cottages Mrs. Bentley had spoken of. They easily found cluster three and parked in the small gravel lot that corresponded with it. Owen opened up the back of the SUV, and everyone found their bags and went into their cottage.

"This is absolutely perfect," said Alice as she carried her suitcase into the cozy bedroom and set it down. "I can't believe this place has been up here for so many years and I never even knew it."

"It's so peaceful," said Luke, looking out the window. He walked to the desk to set down the stack of books Alice had brought and picked up a sheet of paper. "Here's a note from our mysterious host. It says we should get unpacked and then meet in the main building for an afternoon tea by the fireplace. Our host would like to say hello."

Alice was just emerging from the bathroom, where she had brushed out her hair and put on some lipstick, when Owen knocked at the door.

"Can you get over this place?" he said, coming

into their cottage. "We can sit out on our porches and read."

"Or go for walks through the orchards," said Alice. She joined Luke by the window and looked out. "You can almost imagine the monks here back in the day, living in these cottages, tending to their gardens . . ."

"Not a bad life," said Owen. "I think I could get used to this."

"We'd better head over to the main building," said Luke.

"Ah yes! For afternoon tea," said Owen, holding open the door.

They all walked along the stone path that led to the main building, admiring the grounds as they went. When they arrived in the room with the fireplace, Alice noticed another brass plaque posted discreetly on the wall next to a hallway that led out of the room. She walked over to take a closer look.

"Spa, library, office, dining hall . . ." she read. She peered down the hallway, tempted to go and find the library. But it would have to wait until later, since the other guests were arriving and Mrs. Bentley had rolled out an elaborate tea cart, laden with several pots, stacks of China cups and saucers, and a selection of tiny sandwiches and sweets.

Owen accepted his cup of tea and took a bite of a cucumber sandwich. "That woman over there looks very familiar," he said in a low voice. "Does anyone know who she is?"

Alice turned in the direction Owen was looking and immediately knew the woman, who stood by the fireplace wearing a pair of brown slacks and a mustard-colored turtleneck, her dark hair pulled back into a neat bun. "That's Cate Whitaker—the famous mystery author! I can't believe it! I have all of her books at the shop."

"You guessed correctly," said Mrs. Bentley pouring Alice a cup of tea. "Both Cate and her husband, Adam Burns, were invited for the weekend—"

"The first couple of mystery! Both of them are here?" Alice hadn't meant to interrupt, but she was overjoyed at the idea of spending an entire weekend with two of her favorite authors.

Mrs. Bentley handed Alice her cup. "Unfortunately, Mr. Burns was unable to attend."

"Oh," said Alice. "Still! I can't believe I'm going to get to meet Cate Whitaker."

Once they all had tea and had taken a sampling of the tasty tidbits on offer, they moved over to the fireplace and said hello to the other guests.

"I'm a big fan of your work, Ms. Whitaker," Alice said, shaking hands with Cate. "I own a bookshop down in Blue Valley. The Paper Owl. We stock all your books."

"That's wonderful to hear! And please, call me Cate."

Alice was just introducing herself and the whole group of friends when the door opened and a woman walked in and looked around. "This is just beautiful," she said, tucking an unruly honey-colored curl behind her ear. She wore a long skirt in a deep plum color, a flowy blouse in an earthy green, and earrings that dangled almost to her shoulders—the epitome of a free spirit. She noticed the rest of the guests looking her way. "Hello. I'm Juniper. Juniper Straya," she said in a sing-songy voice.

They all introduced themselves and collectively marveled at the place, wondering about their host and how they had been so lucky to be invited up the mountain.

"I'm sure whoever he is, our host is a most generous person," said Cate with a smile that made Alice wonder if the woman already knew the identity of their benefactor.

The door opened again and a man walked in—tall,

lanky, silver-haired. He sized up the room and turned to the group. "Hello." He came forward.

"You look familiar," said Cate, smiling at him. "Have we met before?"

"I don't think so," the man answered. "I just have one of those faces. Of course, I do recognize you, from your book jackets." He gave a little bow, then smiled at Alice, who stood at his right elbow.

"Hi," she said. "You're a guest here too, I take it?" When the man nodded in response, she whispered, "Do you have any idea who owns this place?"

But before he could venture an answer, the door opened yet again and in walked a man who looked to be in his forties, dressed impeccably in a tailored suit, his handsome features offset by hair that was combed back away from his face. He was perfectly turned out in every way except that his left arm was in a sling. He was followed by two men—one in chef's attire and the other in khakis and an olive green shirt and work boots. Mrs. Bentley hurried over to join them.

"Welcome to The Abbey!" the man said in a booming voice. "I'm so pleased you're all here." He flashed a charming smile. "I'm your host, Harrison Huxley."

"Oh my gosh, I've heard of him," Franny whispered to Alice.

"Me too," whispered Owen. "He's fabulously wealthy."

"Why on earth did he invite *us* here?" Alice hissed.

"You're probably all wondering why I invited you here," said Harrison, clasping his hands together. "Please. Take a seat and I'll explain everything." He waited for them all to sit, then started by introducing his staff. "This is Chef Sacha Alard—yes, his reputation precedes him. He recently came to us from Europe where he is credited with bringing the famous *Le Citron* up to three Michelin stars. He has created a wonderful menu for us this weekend, which I know you will all enjoy."

Harrison turned to Mrs. Bentley. "You have all already met our incomparable Mrs. Bentley, I believe? I couldn't run this place without her and wouldn't want to." The older woman blushed and gave a little curtsy. "And if you've noticed our grounds here at The Abbey, you already know that we have a master gardener at the helm—who also happens to be a bona fide horticulturalist. Meet Sully Addison."

Everyone gave the staff a round of applause, then Harrison explained that by the next week, the full staff would be in place, but for the weekend, they would make do with a skeleton crew. He then made the guest introductions.

"Many of you have likely recognized Cate Whitaker on sight. She can weave a mystery like no other author I've ever encountered."

Cate bowed her head graciously.

"And this"—he pointed at the tall, lanky man—"is Levi Spurgeon. He's a retired scientist—a paranormal scientist, to be more specific. He investigates the mysteries of our lives."

Levi, who had been taking a sip of tea when he was introduced, coughed loudly. "Sorry. Went down the wrong way," he said, setting his teacup on the end table.

"This little nymph over here is Juniper Straya, a well-known and highly respected spiritualist. It's been said that she can tap into the spirit world as easily as most of us can take a breath."

Juniper blushed and took a drink of tea.

"This," Harrison said, walking behind Ben's chair to clap his shoulders, "is the chief of police in the nearest town, Blue Valley—and this," Harrison shifted to Luke, "is his chief investigator. The two of them let no crime go unsolved and have brought a small town department up to the highest standards."

Alice noticed that both her brother and her

husband had slightly wary expressions on their faces, but they graciously accepted the compliments.

"I'm beginning to wonder why you assembled us all here," Luke ventured. "I have a feeling it wasn't a random selection."

"I'll get to that in just a moment," said Harrison. "But first, I'd like to introduce these last four guests." He swept an arm toward Alice, Owen, Michael, and Franny. "Michael Boyd, brilliant poet and head concierge at the prestigious Great Grandaddy Mountain Preserve and Resort Lodge—better known as the Lodge. Mr. Boyd knows what you need before you even realize it yourself, *and* he's been instrumental in helping these three"—he pointed at Alice, Owen, and Franny—"to solve countless mysteries in Blue Valley. You wouldn't know it to look at them, but these three people, Alice Maguire-Evans, Owen James, and Franny Brown-Maguire, have become indispensable to the local police force, and I think Captain Maguire and Detective Evans here would be the first to agree."

Both Ben and Luke nodded.

"Absolutely," said Ben. "They're born detectives."

"I've read about them in the paper," said Levi, giving them a small salute. "They've definitely got the knack."

"So." Harrison clapped his hands and went back to stand at the fireplace in front of the entire group. "Why have I assembled a group of people who are gifted in the extraordinary ways that you are gifted? It's quite a story, my friends, and I wouldn't have believed it myself six months ago."

Harrison went on to explain that The Abbey had originally been built and inhabited by a small French brotherhood who had created a working farm on the mountaintop, complete with crops and livestock. They had even created a weekly market where they sold off excess vegetables, eggs, handmade crafts, and the like, and had been famous throughout the region for the soups, sauces, and flavored cooking oils that could be purchased on market days.

"It was also said that there were many relics and treasures of great value that were kept here," Harrison explained. "And that might've been the monks' undoing in the end. One week, a man named Mercurius Snee came up the mountain on a market day. Snee looked around the market, picked a few pockets, and was about to go on his way when he heard some other folks talking about valuable treasures that were stashed away up here. Well, he was determined to steal what he could, so he hatched a scheme. He went back down the mountain and told his band of thieves about what he'd heard. Then he disguised himself as a beggar, and on the next stormy day, made his way back up the mountain, then begged the brothers for assistance. Of course they took him in." Harrison shook his head. "That night, when the brothers had gone to bed, Snee crept out and unlocked the gates, letting in his minions. They ransacked the place—took everything they could find that was worth anything. Thankfully, the monks were smart enough to abandon ship and escaped alive—all of them, that is, save one.

"Brother Auguste refused to leave. He was known for his stubbornness, and holed up in the chapel. Well, Snee and his band of thieves had taken every candlestick, every coin that the monks had earned—down to the very last egg and jar of pickled beets. But as they retreated with their haul, Snee looked back and saw that Brother Auguste was still in the chapel. Being the scoundrel that he was, Snee decided there must be something very valuable in that chapel if the monk was willing to risk his life to guard it. Consumed by greed, he ran back to take whatever it was, and in his haste to search the chapel, knocked over a lantern without noticing it. The place caught fire and both Brother Auguste and Mercurius Snee perished in the blaze.

"The ruins still stand at the back of this property to this day, in a small grove of chestnut trees that the monks had cultivated." Harrison looked at the group. "As many of you know, chestnut trees used to grow by the thousands in these parts, but most of them were lost to blight by the 1940s." He shoved his hands into his pockets. "So now, we come to the present time—and the curse." He nodded. "I know, I know. You're probably mostly too sensible to believe in such things, and so was I."

"I'm not," said Juniper. "Curses can be very real."

"One of the reasons you're here," said Harrison, pointing at her. "Legend has it that this land is cursed. If someone tries to build something or cultivate it or make money from it, Brother Auguste haunts them. If someone disturbs the land or looks for the lost treasure of the brothers, Mercurius Snee goes after them. And I never would've believed in any of this, but now I'm not so sure.

"Strange things have been happening through the entire renovation process, but they're escalating as I get closer to the grand opening. Construction workers have been injured. Materials have gone missing to the extent that the project has been delayed repeatedly. We were supposed to open last spring, and here it is fall. We've seen lights moving through the woods at night. The chapel ruins caught fire one night and we were lucky Sully saw and called for help quickly enough or it might've been destroyed.

"And now, *I'm* starting to feel threatened—ever since I moved into my cottage. You'll notice it, back in the trees, off by itself. It was the abbot's house back in the 1800s. I completely renovated it and modernized it, but tried to honor its history at the same time. Anyway, bad things have been happening to me. First I ate something and got sick enough that I had to go to the hospital. Then I slipped on a broken step and fractured my wrist." He pointed to the sling. "I wake up and find that things in my cottage have been moved around. I lock the gates every night, but then I'll see a light moving through the trees. I'll run out to check, but there's no one there."

Harrison scanned the faces in the room. "I need this thing solved before I open the place. Before I get seriously hurt—or worse. That's why I've brought you here. Each one of you has a gift for unraveling mysteries." He quickly held up his hands. "Now if you don't want to get involved, I understand. I won't force you. You are free to go home or just stay and enjoy yourselves. The weekend will include gourmet meals, breathtaking views, and top notch accommodations. This building we're in now is open twenty-four hours a day, and you are welcome to come here any time to browse our extensive library, grab a snack, or sit by the fire." He paused. "But I'm asking you to consider helping me." He looked out the window at the beautiful view. "The Abbey will be the ultimate exclusive retreat. There will be no billboards or splashy ads leading clients here. Only word of mouth. I want this to be a haven, where guests can truly get away from it all. I would *imagine* that even Brother Auguste would approve of that. But no one will come if word gets out about what's been happening up here. I'll lose my shirt. Then I'll really have to scour this land and find the monks' treasure, whatever it is, just to break even!"

Juniper folded her arms over her chest. "That explains the presence I've sensed here. There is a spirit who wants you to leave."

"Hey, I'm sorry if Brother Auguste and Mercurius Snee want the place left alone, but I've sunk a fortune in this mountaintop. I *have* to do business here."

"You could be killed," Juniper said with a shiver. "The danger is going to escalate. The spirits are restless."

"Don't be ridiculous." Cate Whitaker scoffed at her. "There's got to be a logical explanation for all of this."

Harrison nodded. "I don't know what to believe anymore." He implored them all to give it some thought, then left, reminding them that dinner would be served at seven. The members of the staff trickled out of the room soon after, and before long, mouthwatering smells began to drift out of the kitchen.

"I'm not sure what to do," said Juniper, moving over to stand next to the fire. "Are you all going to stay?"

"Well I am," said Cate. "There's most definitely a book in this somewhere. Might as well stick it out and see what happens."

"I don't know about all this," said Levi. "That Harrison might just have a screw loose. I don't believe in curses."

"But aren't you a paranormal scientist?" asked Franny.

"Well," Levi hesitated. "It's just that most of the time, claims like this turn out to be bogus."

"It's so rare for all of us to get the same weekend off," said Alice, motioning toward her group.

"As in, it *never* happens," added Owen.

"I'm beginning to wonder if Harrison himself had a hand in that," said Alice.

"Like maybe he called all of our helpers and told them to volunteer to work this weekend?" said Owen.

"Harrison is clearly a man who gets what he wants," said Juniper. "He wanted us all here, and here we are."

Alice caught Cate almost glaring at the spiritualist and wondered why there seemed to be tension between the two women. "Did any of you know Harrison before today?" she asked.

All around the room, heads shook. A roll of thunder sounded in the distance.

Levi walked to the window. "Storm's moving in. We should probably all stay put tonight, anyway. That mountain road wouldn't be any fun in the rain."

"My stomach is imploring me to stay," said Owen, patting his belly.

Alice looked at Luke. "Want to give it a night and see how things go?"

Luke brushed a curl out of her face. "A weekend at a luxury resort with you? Sounds pretty good to me."

CHAPTER 4

Everyone dispersed and returned to their cottages to relax and get ready for dinner. A cold front was moving in right along with the rain, so Luke built a fire in their woodstove and he and Alice snuggled up on the couch in their small living room to read. Reading time quickly turned into naptime, and a rumble of thunder woke them about an hour later.

"I can't remember the last time we actually slept until we woke up on our own," said Luke, yawning and stretching.

"I can. Six months ago," said Alice with a laugh. "I never thought I'd be this excited about uninterrupted sleep!"

Half an hour later, they, along with Owen,

Michael, Franny, and Ben, emerged onto their covered porches just as the rain let up.

"Perfect timing," said Owen, eyeing the sky.

But the wind whipped around them as they made their way back to the main building and thunder rolled overhead. Alice wrapped her arms around herself and shivered a little.

"Want me to go back and get your sweater?" Luke asked, putting an arm around her as they walked.

"That's okay. I'll do it," said Alice. "Meet you by the fireplace!" She turned and jogged back to the cottage, ran inside, and grabbed her sweater. As she stepped out onto the porch, there was a clap of thunder that sounded awfully close. She'd need to hurry to beat the rain—or worse, a lightning strike. Unfortunately, she hadn't gone far when the sky opened up and dumped its entire contents. Alice picked up her pace, dodging puddles. She ducked into a small building that lay between the cottages and the main building to wait out the worst of it. She pulled her phone out of her pocket and texted Luke, telling him she was fine and would be along shortly.

Alice caught her breath and bushed a wet strand of hair out of her face. She looked around, wondering if this odd little building was old or new. It appeared to be old—perhaps restored from the days of the original Abbey. It had that smell you can't recreate in a new structure. It reminded Alice of the hiking trail shelters that were scattered around the many trails in the Smokies—open on three sides, but this one had a half wall in the middle with benches built into both sides. Alice took a seat and watched the rain, falling in solid sheets now. She closed her eyes and breathed deeply. The air was so fresh up here on the mountain. She wondered if this structure had been a barn back in the day, or perhaps a place of prayer for the monks, or a place to store goods to be sold on their market days.

What a shame that something so pure and beautiful that only served to help others had come to such a tragic end. The world would be a much nicer place without people like Mercurius Snee spoiling things. Alice heard rapid footsteps approaching—probably someone else trying to get in out of the rain. She started to stand to see who it was, since they were on the other side of the half wall, but then stopped herself when she heard a very upset voice.

"I said no! I won't do it. I'm not some circus sideshow you can bring in when you feel like it!"

There was no mistaking that voice. It was Juniper, the spiritualist. Alice had no idea who she was talking to, and grappled with the idea of making her presence known before anyone said anything that they wouldn't want others to hear.

"Juni, you know I don't think of you that way. You have the gift. I truly believe it. I'd like you to hold a séance. I want you to try to contact the spirits that inhabit this place, to see if I can make peace with them. I need this favor from you. Please consider—"

That voice was a man. By context, it had to be their host, the dashing Harrison Huxley, didn't it? If the rain would only stop pounding so hard, Alice could be sure. She pressed herself up against the wall, wishing she could hide under the bench, and feeling more than a little awkward at this point.

"*I need, I want*! That's all that matters to you! What *you* need and want. Why on earth would you think I owe you a favor?"

"I don't! I didn't mean—"

"I thought you brought me up here because . . . well, because you wanted to get back together."

Alice could hear Juniper's voice crack painfully. There was a pregnant pause.

"No. I—it's not that I don't want . . ." His voice faded. "It's complicated right now. I'm with someone else. But—"

"Do you have any idea how selfish you are?"

"Juni, you are the most amazing woman. It's just that it's—it's complicated."

"Leave me alone!"

Juniper started to run out of the shelter, into the rain. Alice tried to hold her breath and stay perfectly still, because she could actually see the woman now. And if Juniper were to turn back and actually look, she'd be able to see Alice too. But just as the poor woman stepped out into the rain, a hand reached out and grabbed her, pulling her back.

Now there was no doubt that it was Harrison she'd been talking to. Alice could feel her own face flushing as she stayed stock still, praying the two wouldn't decide to look her way and realize she'd heard everything.

That was when Harrison, in one swift movement, pulled Juniper into his arms and kissed her passionately. Alice tried not to gape. It was like a scene in a movie. One of Harrison's hands went to the back of Juniper's head, the other stayed firmly at her waist, and Juniper seemed to go a little limp in his arms before wrapping her own arms around his neck and returning the kiss. But then she pulled abruptly away and glared at him.

"That's not fair."

"But—"

"No!"

"Juni, I'm sorry! It's just . . . I'm truly afraid of what's happening up here. Please—"

"No!"

With that, Juniper ran out of the shelter, into the rain, toward the main building. Alice saw Harrison's shoulders sag, then he walked in the same direction.

Alice waited a few minutes, stunned by what she'd just witnessed and not wanting to follow too closely behind the others. Hadn't Juniper, like all the other guests, said she didn't know Harrison? Clearly, she'd been lying. But why?

The rain had the goodness to lighten just a little, so Alice made a break for the main building.

"There she is!" said Luke as she came into the room with the great stone fireplace. "I was about to come search for you."

"Come stand by the fire," said Owen. "You're all wet."

The whole group of guests was standing around in the room, chatting in little clusters while enjoying a variety of delicious looking appetizers and cocktails.

Franny brought Alice a steaming mug. "Mulled wine," she said. "It'll warm you right up."

"Thanks."

"It's really coming down out there, huh?" said

Cate Whitaker, who was standing in their circle near the fire.

"It is," said Alice, feeling a rush of excitement at being face to face with such a talented author—along with a small wave of embarrassment that while Cate looked beautiful, Alice was a wet mess.

"So you said you own a bookstore in Blue Valley?" asked Cate, who didn't even seem to notice the state of Alice's hair and clothes.

"She does," Owen quickly answered. "The Paper Owl on Main Street. You should come do a book signing sometime. I own the bakery next door and would be happy to provide the food."

"And I could bring the coffee!" said Franny, shifting Owen over a bit with her shoulder. "I own the coffee shop that is also next door to Alice's bookstore."

"That sounds wonderful!" said Cate.

"You mean you'd really consider—" Alice stopped and took hold of herself. She wanted to at least attempt to sound as professional as possible. "I would absolutely love to book you for a signing. You'll find a large fan base in Blue Valley—I'm constantly restocking your books."

"I'll do it," said Cate, smiling and taking a sip from her mug.

"Wow," said Franny, watching as Cate lowered the mug. "Is that your wedding band? It's gorgeous!"

"It is," said Cate, looking down at the ring. "Emeralds are my birthstone, so my husband—well, he wasn't my husband back then . . . He had this made, just for me. Twenty years ago."

"You're married to Adam Burns, right?" said Owen. "You two really are the first couple of mystery, like they say. Two bestselling authors living in the same house! Must be pretty amazing."

Cate paused before answering, and Alice thought she saw the tiniest hint of sadness in the woman's eyes. "Back when we first got married, we were just two young writers, getting our first taste of success. We never could've imagined what our future held."

"Too bad Mr. Burns couldn't come this weekend," said Alice. She took Luke's hand. "This place is a wonderful romantic getaway."

Cate just smiled at that, and then Owen and Michael began asking her about her latest project. Alice let her eyes wander around the room and spotted Juniper, still wet and a little shaken from her run through the rain. She also saw Harrison, talking to Levi off in the corner. The next thing Alice knew, Juniper was going out onto the covered porch that wrapped around the large building. Alice leaned around Owen to see that the spiritualist was standing with her hands on the railing, watching the rain fall. She searched the room for Harrison. He was still talking to Levi, but a few minutes later, he seemed to be excusing himself, and then he, too, went out onto the porch, but not through the same door. Would Juniper see him out there? Alice tried to find her, but she must've moved around to a different stretch of the porch because she wasn't still there at the railing.

"Oh—I've just realized I forgot something in my room," said Cate. "My phone. The rain's let up. I'll be right back." With that, she hurried out the same door Harrison had gone through.

Alice was so caught up in her thoughts about who was where that she hadn't even noticed that Owen had left the room until he came back.

"Where'd you go?" she asked, taking a healthy swig of mulled wine.

"Just popped into the kitchen," said Owen. "I wanted to say hello to Chef Sacha and introduce myself."

"And check out what he's making for dessert, right?" said Michael, nudging him.

"He knows me so well," said Owen, propping an elbow on Michael's shoulder. "Chef and Mrs. Bentley are in the kitchen putting together the most amazing dinner. And I passed through the dining hall on the way to the kitchen. The salads are already plated and on the table, and they look fabulous."

"I can't wait!" said Franny.

Just then, Mrs. Bentley entered the room with a gorgeous arrangement of branches covered in red berries mixed with small pine boughs and colorful fall leaves. She set the arrangement on the fireplace mantle.

"That is amazing!" said Franny. "Did you make that, Mrs. Bentley?"

"Me? No," she answered with a chuckle. "Sully created this along with the centerpieces you'll see on the table in a moment. He knows every plant that grows in this whole region. You'd never know it to look at him, but he's an artist in his own way."

"Definitely!" said Alice.

"I'd like to get some ideas from him for the arrangements we use at the Lodge," said Michael.

"I'm sure he'd be glad to talk plants anytime," said Mrs. Bentley, touching up the arrangement.

Owen leaned over to Alice. "I wonder what happened to Juniper," he whispered. "She looks upset. And she's even wetter than you were."

Alice hadn't noticed that Juniper had returned to

the room. She looked around in search of Cate and Harrison, but just then, Chef Sacha entered.

"If you will all come this way, dinner is served!" he announced.

The group followed him into the dining room, passing Sully as they did. In his hands was a plate covered in tinfoil.

Alice smiled at him. "Your arrangements are just beautiful," she said. "Everyone's talking about them."

He flushed. "Thank you. I enjoy making them."

"Are you coming to dinner?" asked Michael. "I'd love to ask you more about how you create them."

Sully smiled and held up the plate. "Got mine to go. I still have work to do before the day's out." He gave them a polite nod and headed out the main front door.

The dining room was breathtaking. It'd be even better, Alice could see, in the morning. One entire wall was huge windows, almost floor-to-ceiling in height. The views of the mountains and valley would be incredible come morning. Alice noticed that some of the windows were actually doors, and that the wraparound porch even extended to this section of the building. She sighed contentedly, deciding that the next morning, if it wasn't raining, she'd sit outside with her morning coffee and her book.

There were place cards set out on the table. Alice found her seat and admired the salads, which featured a variety of greens, apples, toasted walnuts, ruby red pomegranate seeds, plump blueberries, and savory chunks of blue cheese. They were topped off with homemade crusty croutons and tiny, crisp butternut squash fritters.

"I know you know something," Owen, seated next to Alice, whispered. "And it's a juicy something."

Alice turned wide eyes to him, very aware that Juniper was sitting directly across the table from her. She tried mouthing the word *later*, but Owen thought she was saying *take her* and a short bout of confusion ensued before Alice had no choice but to give him a little kick under the table.

Meanwhile, at the head of the table, Harrison sat, looking a little tense but chatting with his guests and enjoying the salad course. Alice noticed him taking lots of drinks from his water glass, and clearing his throat a good deal, and wondered if he was nervous thinking about Juniper, who he kept glancing toward. Juniper, on the other hand, was ignoring him entirely.

As everyone was finishing up their salads, Harrison stood, wavered a little, put a hand to his forehead, and cleared his throat. "I apologize," he said. "I'm not feeling well and will have to excuse myself." When this was met with concerned looks from his guests, he held up his hands. "No, no—don't worry. Please, enjoy your meal. I look forward to seeing you all tomorrow." With a little bow, he set his napkin on the table and left the room.

Alice watched him go, wondering if his sudden exit had anything to do with Juniper. She looked at the other guests at the table. Most wore expressions of either surprise or concern. Juniper, however, was staring in the direction of the door Harrison had gone through, and Cate was looking away, out the window.

"That's too bad," said Owen. "He didn't even get to the main course."

As if on cue, Chef Sacha, with the help of Mrs. Bentley, came out of the kitchen. When the chef frowned at the empty chair, Levi told him what Harrison had said.

He nodded. "Mr. Huxley, he sometimes has stomach issues." He went on to tell the group about the main course while Mrs. Bentley cleared away the salad plates. Then the two of them brought in dinner plates, laden with roast duck with buttered cabbage and apples, salty rosemary-focaccia bread, and herb-crusted potatoes.

"Save room for dessert," Owen said as they dug in. "Chef has a caramelized pear tart that's to die for in the kitchen." He took a bite of duck with potatoes. "Amazing! What is that flavor?"

Mrs. Bentley, who happened to be walking around the table refilling glasses, grinned. "That's Chef's secret signature ingredient. Even I don't know what it is!"

"It's familiar," said Owen, "but I can't place it." He shrugged. "I'm a pastry chef. What do I know about savory flavors?"

"It's so rich," said Ben. "And that sauce! Wow!"

By the time dessert had been devoured, everyone was leaning back in their chairs, immensely satisfied. They gave the chef a round of applause when he came out of the kitchen and he graciously bowed.

"I will see you all at breakfast in the morning!"

"Your meals for the remainder of the weekend will be served buffet-style, so that you may dine at your leisure," added Mrs. Bentley. "Sleep well!"

After that, the guests dispersed a few at a time. Alice and her group stayed by the fireplace, laughing, and telling stories until the rain lightened up again, so it seemed a good time to head back to the cottages.

"It's after nine. Let's check on the kids, get into our PJs, and meet up in Alice and Luke's cottage for a movie," Owen suggested.

"Sounds perfect!" said Alice.

As they scurried through the drizzle toward their cluster of cottages, a bolt of lightning illuminated the sky. Alice glanced toward the woods, where a slightly larger cottage stood apart from the others. A shadowy figure stood at the door, knocking. Alice stopped for a moment. It was Cate.

"Is that Harrison's cottage, do you think?" she asked, grabbing Franny's arm.

"I think so," said Franny. "It's in the trees, kind of by itself like he described. Plus, I saw him coming out of it earlier today."

"Why is Cate standing on his porch, knocking on his door in this weather?"

Owen, who was looking in the same direction by that time, frowned. "Good question."

A roll of thunder grumbled across the sky. Alice shivered. "None of our business. We'd better get inside."

CHAPTER 5

Alice couldn't remember the last time she'd slept so soundly. Maybe it was because of the steady rain that had tapped on the cottage roof all night. Maybe it was because she'd eaten such a good meal and ended the day winding down with her favorite people in the world. Of course, it might have had something to do with the fact that she knew that Izzy was safe and sound in the care of her grandparents—as opposed to waking Alice up to be fed at all hours.

After a phone call to check in with Bea and Martin, she and Luke got dressed and stepped out onto their porch. The air was clear and cool, the sun breaking through the clouds just above the mountain rims and casting a pink glow over everything.

"What's that old saying? Red sky in the morning,

bees will be swarming?" said Owen, who'd just come out of his own door and was stretching his arms out.

"You *never* remember it correctly!" said Alice. "It's *red sky at morning, sailors take warning*." She looked at Luke. "Right?"

"I think so."

"So that means bad weather later today?" asked Owen.

"Could be," said Alice. "How'd you sleep?"

"Like the proverbial baby," said Owen. "Not like real babies, who, according to you and Franny, are up all night."

"Another confusing idiom," said Alice.

"What time is breakfast?" asked Franny, coming out onto her porch with Ben.

"There's an itinerary on the desk in each cottage. The serving window doesn't start for half an hour," said Alice.

"We have time to take a walk then," said Franny.

"Great idea," said Luke.

They all agreed that they'd like to find the old chapel—haunted or not—so they put on sweaters and jackets and headed off toward the back acreage of the property. As they walked along, they chatted about how well they'd slept and how plush the beds and pillows were.

"The turndown service is excellent," said Michael.

"Yes!" said Owen. "I loved those little shortbread cookies they left by the bed."

"We should do something like that at the Lodge. As of now, we leave chocolate mints. But there's something so comforting about a little cookie."

"How does Mrs. Bentley do it all? That woman really gets around," said Franny.

"She says the full staff arrives next week, and she'll actually be overseeing the housekeeping staff," said Michael. "Apparently Harrison decided to do this pre-opening weekend just over the last few weeks—rushed the fancy invitations and got our cottages ready early to pull it off. So the skeleton staff is doing double or triple duty."

"Well they're doing a wonderful job," said Alice. "Every detail has been attended to."

"So I guess we're all in agreement that we're staying the weekend and looking into the curse?" said Ben, taking Franny's hand.

"It's worth it," said Franny, nodding. "How often do we get to have a luxurious weekend getaway like this? Besides, the whole curse business is intriguing."

As they passed Harrison's cottage, Alice noticed Cate walking around from the other side of it. She spotted Alice, turned on her heel, and walked briskly in the other direction, toward the main building. Alice was just about to mention to the others that this seemed odd, especially since Cate had claimed she'd never met Harrison before this weekend, but then there was a commotion from among the trees in the chestnut grove. It was Sully—and he was running toward them, looking terrified.

"I just saw a grizzly!" he said as he reached them. "Get inside!"

"A grizzly?" said Luke. "But—"

"Sir, I strongly suggest you get inside your cottages or to the main building," said Sully, who hadn't stopped running and was now passing them.

"Okay," Ben called after him. "Thank you!" He turned back to the rest of the group. "Strange."

"Very," agreed Alice. "There's no chance he saw a grizzly bear."

"Why?" asked Luke.

"Oh that's right," said Owen, putting an arm around him and steering him to walk back in the other direction toward the main building. "You, like myself, weren't born here. See, there are no grizzly bears in the Smoky Mountains. Only black bears."

"Well . . . a bear's a bear, right?" said Luke.

"Black bears are very rarely aggressive," said

Alice. "Most of them wouldn't bother you a bit. But then again, it's almost breakfast time, and I'd hate to disturb a bear, no matter what kind."

"I guess Sully knows more about plants than animals," said Luke with a laugh.

When they entered the main building, they were met by the mouthwatering aroma of breakfast, wafting out from the region of the dining room.

"Follow your nose," said Owen, inhaling deeply.

In the dining room, a gourmet breakfast buffet had been set up on the long table they'd dined at the night before, which had been pushed up against the wall, and smaller tables had been set along the windows, offering spectacular views. There were covered dishes of steaming scrambled eggs, hashbrowns studded with sweet onion, platters of fresh fruits and pastries, and crispy bacon. Alice spotted Cate, out on the porch, drinking her coffee. Juniper was chatting with Levi, both of them filling their plates, and Sully was eating quietly while reading a gardening magazine at a corner table that Alice imagined had been set aside for staff members. Alice and company served themselves and then found seats at a table next to the window.

"There it is again," said Owen after taking a bite of his eggs. "That flavor."

"Chef Sacha's signature ingredient?" said Franny, taking a bite. "Mmm. Delicious."

"We should try to get him to tell us what it is," said Michael.

Thunder rolled outside.

"Looks like we'll have to put our walk off a little longer," said Alice. "It's starting to rain again." She was already deciding which one of the books she'd brought along to read by the fireplace when Mrs. Bentley rushed into the room, red in the face and panting.

"I need help!"

Everyone in the room jumped up at once.

"What's happening?" asked Alice.

"I just went to tidy Harrison's cottage while he was at breakfast. I knocked, to be sure he'd already gone, but"—she put a hand over her heart—"he's still in bed and I can't wake him. Please, come at once!"

Ben and Luke, who were certified and extensively trained in CPR and first aid, led the way, but the whole group followed Mrs. Bentley back to Harrison's cottage, including Cate, who had just come into the dining room to refill her coffee cup. Mrs. Bentley opened the cottage door and stood aside.

"Please stay here," Ben said, turning back briefly.

"We'll assess the situation and let you all know what's happening."

Alice watched her brother and husband disappear into the cottage. She was tempted to peer into the windows out of curiosity. The minutes dragged on before Luke finally came out, followed by Ben.

"Everyone, let's all go back to the main building," Luke announced. "Captain Maguire and I have called an ambulance."

"An ambulance?" asked Cate, panic rising in her voice. "Is Harrison in serious condition?"

"I'd rather we all went back to—"

"Please!" said Juniper. "What's happened? Something is very wrong—I can feel it."

Luke sighed and looked at Ben, who gave a small nod. "I'm afraid Mr. Huxley is dead."

CHAPTER 6

Ben and Luke called everyone together in the main building, inviting them to make themselves comfortable on the couches and chairs while they waited for the ambulance to arrive.

After only a few minutes, a teary-eyed Cate stood to go. "I'm going back to my cottage. I'm tired and would like to lie down."

Luke stepped in front of the door. "I understand, Ms. Whitaker. But for now, I'll need you to stay in this room along with everyone else."

He'd used his detective voice, Alice noticed. When Luke took that tone, people generally didn't question him, and neither did Cate, who sat back down with a sniff.

Chef Sacha and Mrs. Bentley were permitted to

go into the kitchen to brew a fresh pot of coffee, but otherwise, people either wandered to look out the windows or talked quietly amongst themselves. It was raining steadily now, and Alice thought of the ambulance, fighting its way up the narrow, winding—and now very muddy and slippery—mountain roads to get to them. When the coffee was served, she poured a cup for Luke, who was standing at the main door to the building, watching for the paramedics to arrive.

"Thanks," he said, taking a sip.

"This wasn't an accidental death, was it?" whispered Alice.

Luke looked at her over the rim of his mug, but didn't answer.

"That's why you're keeping everyone here. There's something suspicious about the way Harrison Huxley died."

Luke sighed. "Okay," he whispered. "You're about to find out anyway. I was just holding off until Doc gets here. We talked on the phone, but I'd like him to have a look at the body to confirm what he already suspects based on what we found. And of course, Zeb Clark, the coroner, will have to do a full examination when they get the body down the mountain."

"What you found—"

"Harrison had been really sick before he died, but just a few hours before that when he welcomed us all here, he displayed no symptoms and seemed to feel great. And remember, he appeared dizzy when he got up from the table last night."

"He was clearing his throat a lot, too!"

Luke nodded. "Doc says he's almost certain he was poisoned. Most likely last night."

"He left dinner after eating his salad," whispered Alice. "He didn't feel well!"

Luke nodded.

"Someone—" Alice stopped and glanced around, then lowered her voice even further. "Someone poisoned his salad?"

"It's a possibility. According to Doc, it would be very easy to hide something like the leaves or berries of a nightshade plant in a salad, and Harrison's symptoms are consistent with those of someone who consumed that particular toxin. Plus it can be found around here pretty easily."

Alice felt a nervous knot in her stomach as she rejoined Franny, Owen, and Michael on the couch.

Owen elbowed her. "What's up?"

Alice shot him a look, hoping he'd drop the subject. Instead, he elbowed her again.

Finally Alice leaned close to Owen's ear and whispered, "Poison."

Owen's eyes fairly popped out of his head. "Seriously?"

Alice gave a quick nod. "Doc is coming to confirm."

"If he can get up here on those roads," said Owen. "Trust me—I drove them yesterday when it was dry. It was harrowing enough then!"

"They should've been here by now, don't you think?" said Michael.

Alice looked across the way to where Cate was now standing, looking out the window. On closer inspection, Alice realized that Cate's shoulders were trembling. The woman was sobbing! Alice nudged Owen and then nodded in Cate's direction.

Owen leaned over to Michael. "Hand me that quilt," he said, pointing to the quilt that had been draped over the arm of the sofa.

Michael handed him the quilt, and he and Alice walked over to Cate.

"You look chilled. Thought you could use this," said Owen.

Cate took the blanket and wrapped it around herself. "Thanks." She sniffled, and Alice handed her a tissue. She blew her nose.

On the other side of the room, Ben's phone rang. Alice glanced over at her brother, hoping he was hearing from the paramedics about why it was taking them so long to get here. She turned back to Cate. "Cate, is there anything we can do? You seem very upset."

"Of course you are," Owen added quickly. "It's upsetting that our host died such an untimely death."

"Shocking," said Cate in a trembling voice.

"Do you know whether or not he had any serious health conditions, by any chance?"

Cate turned her bloodshot eyes to Owen. "How would I know that?"

Owen shrugged. "I don't know, I just thought . . . maybe . . ."

"Well I don't. As far as I could tell, Harrison seemed to be a very healthy man. Perfectly healthy. Too young to—" She looked over at the main door that Luke was still guarding. "I'm leaving. They can't make me stay." With that, she began to walk across the wood floor.

But before she was even halfway across the room, Ben clicked off of the call he'd just received. He turned to the group. "I just heard from the ambulance. Unfortunately, they're having a hard time getting through. It's going to be a little while before they can get here, so if you'll all just bear with us—"

"No!" said Cate, resuming her quest toward the door. "I'm leaving right now."

"Ms. Whitaker, you can't—" Luke started to say.

"If Levi can leave, then I can too!" said Cate, shifting from sad to angry.

"Levi—" Luke turned in the direction that Cate was pointing. Everyone else did, too. Sure enough, a car with Levi at the wheel, was headed down the driveway.

"Stop him!" said Luke, throwing open the door and running out into the rain.

Ben ran behind him, and pretty much everyone else followed, running down the drive in hot pursuit of the brown sedan. By the time they arrived at the front gate, the car was already edging down the steep descent just beyond it—and sliding along in the mud. The wheels locked and the car continued to slip downward, perilously close to the edge of the road, which was also the edge of the mountainside. A few more yards and Levi could be in for a lot of trouble. Clearly he was stomping on the brakes, and finally, in a desperate attempt to save himself, had the wherewithal to steer the car into the trunk of a large tree that grew beside the road, its roots cascading down the side of the hill.

It worked. The car stopped, the engine was cut, and Levi jumped out and hurried back to the road, badly shaken.

"That was a close call, Mr. Spurgeon," said Ben, taking him by the arm and leading him back toward the abbey's gate. "Let's get in out of this rain."

Levi nodded mutely and went along. It was drizzling lightly again, rather than pouring, thankfully. The whole group trouped back toward the main building. Alice, Owen, Franny, and Michael bringing up the rear.

"So the ambulance can't get up here," said Owen, taking off his jacket and holding it over his head.

"And we can't get down," said Franny.

Alice nodded. "We're stuck here. In paradise. With a killer."

CHAPTER 7

Everyone was allowed to go back to their cottages and change into dry clothes. The storms were scattered, and as Alice emerged onto her porch, she saw a glorious rainbow over the mountains, jutting through a break in the clouds.

"Okay, folks, let's get back over to the main building," Ben said, guiding the group down the main path.

Once inside, Luke stoked up the fire and Mrs. Bentley set out a fresh pot of coffee and a plate of shortbread cookies.

"I had hoped the ambulance would have been able to get here by now," Luke told the assembled group. "They'll keep trying. But in the meantime, it's only fair that we come clean with you about what's going on—especially since we need to get our investigation underway."

"Investigation?" said Cate.

"I saw this coming," said Juniper, folding her hands in her lap.

"You did not!" Cate glared at her.

Juniper stood up, fists on her hips. "What is your problem with me, anyway? I haven't done anything to you!"

"Stop trying to act like you know what's going on any more than the rest of us do!"

"Hey—anyone can know what's going on if they'll just be still and listen to the voices around us. It's not my fault you're too caught up in yourself to sense what's obvious to me!"

"Okay, okay!" said Luke, stepping in. "As I was saying, we will be investigating Mr. Huxley's death. The reason for this is that the circumstances surrounding his death are suspicious, and we need to rule out foul play. The ambulance will arrive as soon as possible, and Doc Howard with it. When that happens, we'll be able to accurately estimate time and cause of death. But let me make myself clear. Until we prove otherwise, we will be treating this death as a murder. And for that reason, no one is to leave here." His gaze settled on Levi and Cate. "Is that clear?"

Everyone nodded.

"We're going to be speaking with each one of you in the dining room, one at a time," said Ben. "Until we call your name, just relax. Go down the hall to the library and get a book, have some coffee. We'll call you when it's your turn."

They started with Chef Sacha, so that he'd be free to get back into the kitchen to work on lunch.

Once they'd disappeared into the dining room, Alice turned to Levi, who was seated in an armchair next to the sofa. "Are you okay? Did you get hurt in the accident?"

Levi sighed. "No. My pride is a little bruised. And my car is pretty banged up. Thank you for asking."

"Why were you trying to get away?" asked Cate, who was seated in the armchair to Levi's right.

"I see that suspicious look on your face," Levi said. "So before you decide I killed Harrison, let me assure you that I didn't."

"Then why were you hightailing it out of here like that?" Cate pressed.

Levi paused and fell back into his chair. "I got spooked, about the curse."

"I thought you didn't believe in the curse," Cate countered.

"Well that was before anyone was dead."

The two looked steadily at each other for another beat before Ben poked his head out of the dining room.

"Ms. Whitaker?"

Cate stood, tossed Levi another skeptical look, and went off to the dining room, glancing with narrowed eyes at Juniper, who was getting a cup of coffee and talking with Michael and Mrs. Bentley, along the way. Juniper returned a glower at Cate, and Michael looked over at Owen, raising his brows.

"I've read about you three," Levi said.

"All good I hope," said Owen.

"You've been in the paper quite a few times for helping the police solve murders around these parts. I'm from Pigeon Forge, and the stories have even started to be carried by our paper." He gave them a salute. "You three would make great private investigators. You have the knack, like I said before. Not everyone does."

Alice glanced at Owen and Franny, then back at Levi. "We try to help out when we can."

"We can't seem to stop ourselves," said Owen.

"Yep," said Franny. "If there's a mystery afoot, we have to butt in."

Levi smiled. "That's how I started out, way back when." He took a sip of his coffee.

Alice frowned. "Started out doing what? Pursuing your study of the paranormal?"

Levi chuckled and checked that no one else was listening. He lowered his voice. "Harrison was always pinning ridiculous occupations on me." He shook his head. "Once, he introduced me as head zookeeper at the Chattanooga Zoo—said I specialized in chimps."

Owen leaned forward. "So what do you do, really?"

"I'm a PI. *Not* retired. *Not* a paranormal scientist, whatever that is. I've worked for Harrison for years, checking things out for him whenever he needed something investigated—and for a man like him, that meant pretty steady work for me."

"But it makes perfect sense for an investigator to have been invited this weekend to help solve the mystery of the curse. Why would Harrison lie about what you do?"

"Oh, I don't know," said Levi. "Maybe he was afraid that people with things to hide get uncomfortable around private investigators. Maybe he wanted everyone to come here with their guards down."

Franny frowned. "But he didn't lie about what Ben and Luke do . . ."

"Come on, Levi," said Owen with a grin. "Tell us the truth. Why were you in such a rush to get out of here when you knew there would be an investigation into Harrison's death?"

Levi blew out a long breath. "Okay. You want to know why? The reason I was trying to escape this mountaintop is because I was afraid Cate Whitaker would kill me. Just like she probably killed Harrison."

CHAPTER 8

Levi didn't feel comfortable discussing the matter any further with Cate giving her statement right in the next room, so Alice asked Mrs. Bentley to tell Ben and Luke they were stepping outside for a few minutes to check on Levi's car, and that he was with them. Once they arrived at the old brown sedan, Levi flipped on his cellphone flashlight and squatted to peer under the car.

"If it weren't so darn muddy I'd crawl under there," he said, shining the light this way and that. "Huh. Doesn't look like the brake lines have been cut or anything. No fluid leaking." He went around to the driver's side and popped the hood open, then took a look inside. "Everything looks fine in here too." He chuckled. "When I was sliding down the mountain, I was afraid maybe someone had tampered with the car, but it looks like it was just the road conditions that caused the whole thing. That's a relief."

"You said you're afraid Cate would kill you," said Alice. "Why?"

Levi looked at her thoughtfully, as though deciding how much to say. "My gut instinct about people is infallible. And I can tell you three are okay, so I'm going to come clean with you, but it stays between us, got it?"

Alice, Owen, and Franny all nodded.

"She said she thought she'd seen me before. I bet you caught that, didn't you?"

More nods.

"Well that's because she has. I've been tailing her for a while now—at Harrison's request." He looked at the ground and kicked a rock. "That's the real reason he introduced me as a paranormal scientist, if you want to know the truth. He didn't want Cate to realize she'd glimpsed me in several places and put two and two together. She's a smart woman. If he'd told everyone my true occupation, how hard would it be for her to figure out that Harrison was having her followed?"

"But why would she want to kill *you*?" asked Franny. "Just for following her around?"

"Did you discover something about her that she wanted to keep secret?" asked Owen.

"Well, let's just say I knew something, as did Harrison, that she wanted to keep secret," said Levi.

"So that's why you suspect she killed him," said Owen.

"But I don't understand," said Alice. "What's Cate's big secret that would be worth killing for?"

Levi looked at the three of them, glanced around, and lowered his voice. "She and Harrison have been having an affair for the past year." He glimpsed their shocked faces. "That's right. It's true. It was a whirlwind thing—he was in Hawaii looking at a commercial property that was coming on the market, she was there at a writer's conference. Same hotel." He rolled his eyes. "They fell in love." He put air quotes around the last two words. "So, Harrison decided he wanted to marry Cate. But as you know, she's got a very high profile marriage."

Franny nodded. "She and Adam Burns. Mystery's first couple."

"Right, right. So it was complicated for her to just up and leave and it could mean a lot of bad press if she didn't handle it right. That's what she told Harrison. Well, time passed, and Harrison started getting impatient. Why was she putting him off? They were in love and wanted to spend their lives together." He paused and leaned in. "And in case you hadn't noticed, Harrison generally got what he wanted when he wanted it."

"A perk of being fabulously wealthy," said Owen.

"Exactly. Everything was a game to Harrison. He was always pulling a million strings in a million different directions. And Cate . . ."—he shook his head—"she wasn't willing to jump when Harrison said jump. So naturally, he started to wonder if she was serious about making a real commitment to him. I can assure you, he was not up for being strung along. Truth is, I think he was about at the end of his rope with Cate, and thinking of breaking it off, but she didn't know that. He actually did invite her up here because she has such a way with weaving and unravelling mysteries—he actually invited her husband as well, in part because he has that same gift." He snickered. "In part, I think, just to rattle Cate's cage."

"So Cate didn't know Harrison was thinking of breaking it off with her, right? So why would she kill him then?" asked Alice.

"Because he was threatening to go public," said Levi. "He'd made his wishes very clear. And Cate, well, she knew what the ramifications could be to her career—not to mention her marriage. That's why I think she had motive to do away with him—he could've ruined her at the drop of a hat, and let's be honest: it wouldn't have affected *his* reputation all that much. Everybody already thinks of him as a playboy. He's a hot commodity on the marriage market."

Alice nodded. "Charming, handsome, worldly—"

"And wealthy beyond belief," said Owen.

"I figure if Cate connects the dots and figures out who I am and what I've been doing, she'll need to get rid of me, too." He shook his head and looked out over the mountains. "I'm not half as afraid of any old curse as I am of a woman on a mission."

"Well this explains why Cate pretended not to know Harrison," said Alice. "She was just doing her darndest to cover up that affair until she made up her mind about her marriage."

"It also explains why she was *so* upset about Harrison's death," said Franny. "I mean, we're all upset—"

"But she's heartbroken," said Owen. "We saw her standing outside Harrison's door last night, you know."

"You did?" Levi straightened. "What was she doing?"

"Knocking," said Alice. "But we didn't see him open the door."

Levi scratched his head. "That puts her in the right place at the wrong time if Harrison was killed last night."

"She was lurking around his cabin again this morning," said Alice. "Why would she do that if she'd already killed him? Oh!" She put a hand to her forehead. "I never did get to tell you the other strange thing I saw last night! We were all going to the main building for dinner, and I ran back to the cottage to grab my sweater."

Alice went on to tell them all what she'd witnessed happening between Harrison and Juniper.

"Are you kidding me?" said Owen. "How could you keep something that scandalous to yourself?"

"Because the woman was sitting right across from me at dinner," said Alice. "And then we had such a nice evening, I just didn't think about it later."

"Harrison had a pretty long relationship with Juniper Straya," said Levi, nodding. "He broke it off shortly before he took that trip to Hawaii. In fact, I think Cate was his rebound romance, but that's just me."

Franny looked at Alice. "So Juniper said she'd thought that Harrison was inviting her up here this weekend because he wanted to rekindle their romance?"

"Yep," said Alice.

Owen whistled. "And he shut her down. So it could've been Cate who killed Harrison . . . or it just as likely could've been Juniper. Classic motive for murder—a woman scorned!"

"Scorned?" said Alice. "You didn't see that kiss."

CHAPTER 9

Back in the main building, the last of the statements were taken and everyone was allowed to return to their cottages while Ben kept an eye on the drive just in case anyone else decided to hop into their car and attempt to drive down the mountain.

Alice sat down next to Luke at the fireplace in the large building. "How's it going so far? Any leads?"

"Not exactly. We've put together a rough timeline. The chef and the housekeeper were in the kitchen together, so they vouched for each other, and Owen popped in there to check on dessert, so he was able to confirm that he'd seen them. Otherwise, no one has a solid alibi for the timeframe we're looking at. The salads were set out on the table around six thirty. We were called in to dinner a little after seven. If Doc's suspicions are correct, and Harrison's salad was poisoned, that means that someone doctored up Harrison's salad during that thirty-minute period."

"We were all in the building together, having appetizers by the fire," said Alice.

"Yes, but think about it. Was everyone there, present and accounted for, the entire time?"

"Oh. You're right. People came and went. I remember Juniper going outside. I think Harrison did too."

"Yep. And someone saw Cate go out as well. Someone could've stepped into the dining room without anyone registering it. Or they could've gone right out the front door, walked around to that side of the building, and entered the dining room through one of those big glass doors. Easy."

"Maybe we're making this too complicated," said Alice. "Maybe the chef poisoned the salad. He made it, after all."

Luke shook his head. "Mrs. Bentley was with him that whole time. The greens had been mixed up in a large bowl to be dressed, and the two of them plated the salads together from that. Then they added the toppings She swears there was no difference between the contents of the plates, and since no one else got sick—"

"The poison had to have been added to Harrison's salad after it was already on the table."

"Right."

Alice looked around, making sure she and Luke were still alone in the room. "Did Levi tell you about his true occupation?"

"Yep," said Luke. "Although I was already suspicious of his career as a paranormal scientist."

"Did he tell you about Cate? And Juniper?"

Luke frowned at her. "No. But to be fair, we didn't ask him about either of them. What are you talking about, Alice?"

Alice quickly filled him in on Harrison's romantic liaisons, and Luke's eyebrows went up. "Well that does shed some light on a few things—and it gives us our first two viable suspects. Good work, my beautiful investigator." He leaned over and kissed her. "Have I ever told you how brilliant I find you?"

Alice giggled. "Yes. But feel free to tell me again any time."

The front door opened and Owen, Michael, and Franny came in.

"Something smells amazing," said Owen. "Is it lunchtime yet?"

"Way past," said Franny.

"Chef has a late lunch ready in the dining room,"

Mrs. Bentley announced, breezing into the room. "Come help yourselves!"

"As dark as it's getting outside, you'd think it was dinnertime," said Alice.

"Another storm's rolling in," said Ben, who'd come inside after Levi, Cate, and Juniper.

"Was that thunder I just heard, or Franny's stomach growling?" said Owen, earning him a swat on the arm from Franny.

They turned to follow the rest of the group into the dining room, but were stopped short by a blood curdling scream coming from the front door. Sully had just run in, out of breath, a look of sheer terror on his face.

"The chapel! It's on fire! Hurry!"

CHAPTER 10

Since there was little hope of getting a fire engine up the mountain in time to save the chapel, it was all hands on deck as they doused the flames. Thankfully, the ground, vegetation, and the chapel itself were all rain-soaked, so the fire was unable to spread, and was quickly well in hand.

"It just came out of nowhere," a very shaken Sully said. "I didn't hear any thunder. Couldn't have been a lightning strike." He shivered. "It's the curse. I know it. I want off this mountain. We should all try to get out of here."

"We had better walk through the chapel and be positive there are no live embers anywhere," Mrs. Bentley said, patting Sully on the back. Sully nodded and the two went into the ruins.

"I don't see how this could've happened," Ben said in a low voice, surveying the site. "There's no electricity in the old chapel, so it wasn't an electrical fire . . ."

"And like Sully said, we're on a break in the rain right now"—Luke glanced at the sky—"I mean, that next storm is clearly looming, but this fire couldn't have been caused by a lightning strike."

"Well it couldn't have been caused by a curse either," said Ben. "Let's go talk to Sully and get more details. Maybe it started earlier and has been simmering for a while."

Ben and Luke followed Sully and Mrs. Bentley into the chapel.

"Let's go with them," said Owen. "Maybe we'll find the lost treasure of the brotherhood!" He and Franny linked arms and trotted off toward the chapel, with Alice and Michael lagging just behind.

"Hey," Michael whispered, grabbing Alice's arm. "What's Chef Sacha up to?"

Alice spotted the chef, taking out his cellphone and briskly walking a distance away from the group. "He looks very concerned," she said. "I wonder if he's spooked about the curse, like Sully."

They watched Sacha duck behind a large tree, putting his phone to his ear as he did so. Alice grabbed Michael by the arm, and the two of them hurried quietly over to stand near the tree, trying to look as casual as possible so that they wouldn't be noticed. Luckily, the other guests had followed Owen's lead and were touring the chapel ruins.

"Walter, it's Sacha Alard. How are things down in the valley today?" There was a pause.

Alice and Michael looked at each other.

"Walter Babbage, do you think?" whispered Alice. He was the only Walter she could think of at the moment who lived in Blue Valley. He owned a real estate firm there.

"No, no, listen to me," Sacha was saying in a low voice. "I am no longer interested in purchasing the property. I'm out."

"They're talking real estate! It's *got* to be Walter Babbage," Michael hissed.

Sacha spoke again. "There's just too much, I don't know, *strangeness* up here." He paused as Walter responded on the other end of the line. "Okay. I'll think about it. But I deserve a deep discount on this godforsaken place if I buy it. For one thing, I think it really is cursed. For another, you get stuck here when it rains. However much money Harrison sank into it, it was too much!" He paused. "We don't even know who technically owns it now, anyway, do we?"

Michael elbowed Alice. "Sacha is thinking of buying this place. I'm shocked."

"Hold on. If he's after The Abbey, couldn't that have been a motive to get rid of the current owner?"

"Absolutely." Michael frowned. "But remember, Sacha has an alibi for around the time when the salad would've been poisoned. Mrs. Bentley."

From the other side of the tree trunk, they heard Sacha say, "Okay. Talk later."

Alice and Michael leaped behind a large bush just as the chef slipped out of his hiding place and walked back to rejoin the group at the chapel. They waited a moment, then followed.

"Let's all go back," Sacha was telling the group when they arrived. "I have a delicious meal all prepared. It was going to be a late lunch, but it has become an early dinner. I'm sure you're famished by now."

The whole group headed back toward the main building, talking quietly among themselves. Levi caught up with Alice, Owen, Michael, and Franny.

"So the question is, how did that fire start?" he said in a low voice.

"Oh believe me, that's not the only question," said Alice. "Michael and I just overheard a conversation between Chef Sacha and Walter Babbage." She looked at Levi. "He's a realtor in Blue Valley."

"I know who he is," said Levi with a nod. "He handled the purchase of this property for Harrison."

Alice and Michael went on to relate what they had heard.

"So now that Harrison's out of the way, the chef is trying to get this place for a steal," said Owen. "Yep. That sounds pretty fishy to me." He paused. "Hold on. How do you buy a thing from a dead person?"

"I guess this place is considered part of Harrison's estate," said Michael. "So you'd presumably have to buy it from his heir."

"Whoever that is," said Franny. "It's not like he planned to die at such a young age. I wonder if he even has a will or has named an heir."

"I can answer that," said Levi. "It's a simple matter because Harrison wasn't married, had no children, and only has one living relative—his mother's sister, Betty."

"Betty?" asked Alice.

"Betty Bentley."

"Mrs. Bentley?" asked Owen. "As in . . . *Mrs. Bentley*?" He pointed up ahead of them, to where the rest of the group had just disappeared into the main building.

"Didn't Harrison introduce her as his aunt?" said Levi. Then he shook his head. "Probably not. He was a strange one sometimes. Very private about the details of his life."

"Why didn't you point this out to us sooner, Levi?" asked Alice. "I mean, doesn't it seem like inheriting a place that's worth a fortune would be a motive for murder?"

"Oh absolutely," said Levi. "But Mrs. Bentley had an alibi, remember?"

Owen nodded. "That's right. Chef Sacha." He snorted. "I mean, either one of those two could've wanted Harrison dead, if you think about it." He waved his arms around. "This place is worth a small fortune. Chef wanted to buy it, and Mrs. Bentley inherits it. If they weren't each other's alibi, we'd have two very viable suspects!" He sighed dramatically. "But I saw them together in the kitchen, so I guess they were telling the truth about all that."

"Oh my gosh." Something had been niggling at Alice's thoughts, just outside the circle of her memory, since earlier that day when Luke had explained the likely murder timeline to her. It came to her now, all at once. "The arrangements!"

Owen frowned. "The—"

"The arrangements that Sully created—the ones Mrs. Bentley set out before dinner last night!"

"They were gorgeous," said Franny.

"Yes, but that's not the point. We all saw Mrs. Bentley setting them out. There were two on the dining table and she brought a third one and placed it on the mantle." She stopped walking and looked at them. "Don't you see? She *had* to have left the kitchen, at least for a while, to set those arrangements out. So there were at least a few moments when Chef Sacha and Mrs. Bentley were apart, and each of them was alone."

Franny swallowed. "Long enough to sprinkle a few nightshade leaves or berries into a salad, easily."

Owen cleared his throat. "Suddenly, I'm not all that hungry."

CHAPTER 11

The sun had almost completely set by the time they'd eaten. The buffet dinner had been delicious—and thankfully, not poisoned in any way. Alice had quickly and quietly informed Luke that there was a hole in Chef Sacha's alibi as well as Mrs. Bentley's. Luke, knowing that they had a very hungry group of people on their hands, had quickly come up with an idea. He cleverly made a toast to the chef before plates were loaded at the buffet, and had then insisted that the chef be the first to eat, followed by the staff.

Sacha had tried to resist, but had then bowed graciously, filled his plate, and was seen digging in at the staff table in the corner. Alice breathed a sigh of relief and enjoyed the meal immensely. Then, since Ben had received word that the ambulance was finally managing to get up the mountain, everyone adjourned to the large front porch of the main building to watch for its arrival.

"Thank goodness!" said Cate, standing at the railing. "Maybe they can figure out what's happened and we'll all finally be able to get out of here!"

Soon, the Blue Valley ambulance pulled into the driveway and parked. Rudy Meyers, a local paramedic, hopped out from the driver's side of the cab, and the coroner, Zeb Clark, stepped out of the passenger's side. Doc Howard swung open the rear door and jumped down.

Alice could've hugged Doc on sight. There was something unfailingly comforting about the man who had delivered half the population of Blue Valley—including both Alice and her own baby. Even in the present dire circumstances, Doc wiggled his bushy eyebrows and made Alice smile.

"How's everyone holding up?" he asked.

"Better now that you're here," said Ben.

"That road needs to be improved before the big opening," said Rudy. "We have to be able to get emergency vehicles up here." He looked around. "Whoa. This place is amazing!"

"And cursed," said Owen, raising a finger.

"Let's have a look at the body," said Zeb. "I'd be

willing to bet a curse had nothing to do with the cause of death."

Doc turned to Ben and Luke. "Lead the way."

"You're all free to stay here or return to your cottages," Ben announced to the group. "We have another set of officers who were able to follow the ambulance up. They'll be guarding the gate tonight. Like we've been saying, another round of storms is moving in, so please do be careful."

With that, the five men walked toward the abbot's house to examine Harrison's remains.

"Let's go get into our PJs," said Franny. "We can meet up at Alice's and watch a movie until Ben and Luke get back."

"Then we can pick their brains," said Michael, rubbing his hands together.

"Excellent plan," said Alice.

A few minutes later, they all reconvened in Alice and Luke's cottage, everyone cozy and comfortable in their sweats and t-shirts and fuzzy socks.

"Before we start the movie, I want to make a quick phone call," said Alice, picking up her cell phone.

"Don't worry. I already checked on the kids for the millionth time today," said Franny.

"Uh, we checked on them too," said Owen.

"Actually, we were checking on Bea and Martin," said Michael. "We were afraid they were beat, what with two little ones and three pets in the house. But it sounds like they're all having the time of their lives. Franny's parents are over helping with bath and bedtime."

"They actually told me to stop calling," said Alice, rolling her eyes. "They said they just want to play with the kids and that we should stop bugging them." She dialed a number on her mobile. "But that's not the phone call I'm talking about. I'm calling Walter Babbage, and I'll put him on speakerphone."

Everyone knew that Walter Babbage would answer the phone any day of the week, any hour of the day, whether he was in the office or in the bathtub. It was part of being Blue Valley's number one realtor, he always said.

"Alice!" Walter said, picking up on the second ring. "Hey—aren't you up on the cursed mountain? Is everything okay up there? You wouldn't believe the rumors going around town!"

"Things are better now that the ambulance has arrived," said Alice. "You're on the speaker, Walter. I'm here with Owen, Michael, and Franny."

Everyone said their hellos and answered Walter's

most pressing questions about what had transpired at The Abbey.

"Norman McKenzie heard there's a ghost up there who's already taken several victims, but I told him that was just nonsense," said Walter.

"Only one victim," Alice assured him. "And there's no ghost."

"Just a coldblooded murderer," said Owen.

"I'm not sure which is worse," said Walter. "When can you get back down here?"

"Who knows," said Owen. "It's starting to rain again and apparently the road is none too friendly right now. I think the ambulance will have to stay the night at this rate."

"Lucky we have two, then," said Walter. "Not that we have too many emergency calls on the average day."

"Walter, we overheard something earlier and I wanted to ask you to help clarify some confusion," said Alice.

"Sure, if I can," said Walter.

"Has someone talked to you about buying The Abbey recently—as in *today*?"

There was a pause. "I can tell you that I have had some interest, but I can't give you any names. It's all premature anyway, since the property is not on the market right now. You know, that place was available for years and years, and no one ever stayed on the hook until Harrison Huxley bought it. People would be interested, go up and look around, and fall in love . . . but then something always happened to change their minds." He chuckled. "I'm not really one for spooky curses, but as far as the real estate market is concerned, trust me, that place is cursed. Every sale had fallen through before Mr. Huxley. Every buyer other than him had been scared away for one reason or another."

There was a knock on Alice's door.

"Thanks Walter. We'll talk later!" she said, ending the call. "Who could that be?"

A peek out the window answered that question. It was Mrs. Bentley.

"Would you like turndown service?" she said with a smile. "I'm so sorry I didn't get it done during dinner, but with the fire and all—"

Alice opened the door and let the woman in. "Mrs. Bentley don't worry about it! We hardly expect turndown service with things such a mess!"

"No, no. Harrison insisted. And I'm sure he'd want you to have as nice a stay as possible, considering." She scurried into the bedroom, turned down the spread, and set a plate of cookies on the nightstand.

"I'm sure Harrison would be very pleased with your work," said Franny.

Tears sprang to Mrs. Bentley's eyes. "That poor boy." She sniffled and then took out a tissue and blew her nose. "Would you like extra towels? Or soaps?"

"No, that's okay," said Alice, laying a comforting hand on the housekeeper's arm. "Would you like to sit down?"

Mrs. Bentley smiled. "I'll be fine." She tucked the tissue into her pocket.

"Mrs. Bentley, before you go—" Alice said quickly, then glanced at her friends.

Owen stood "Mrs. Bentley, please. Sit a while. You look heartbroken."

"Well, that's because I am," she answered, following Owen to the couch and taking a seat. "Harrison was my only . . . my only—"

"Family?" asked Michael.

Mrs. Bentley looked at him. "You knew we were related? Harrison didn't like to tell people that. He always said that family business was private. I supposed the rest of my housekeeping staff would think he only hired me because I was his aunt, and maybe that would cause resentment. But it's not like it was a secret or anything." She sighed. "We just didn't broadcast it."

"Mrs. Bentley," Owen said gently. "We know that as Harrison's only living relative, you inherit the Abbey along with the rest of his estate—"

"What? No! You're mistaken!"

"But—"

"No, I mean you really are mistaken," said Mrs. Bentley. "Harrison and I have talked about this. He left everything to charity."

"He did?" asked Alice. "How generous."

"Yes, he was." Mrs. Bentley took her tissue out again and dabbed at her eyes. "He would've gladly left it all to me—not that either of us ever imagined I'd outlive him. I asked him not to." She smiled. "I have everything I need and more. I had only taken this job to help Harrison." A tear rolled down her cheek. "I can't believe he's gone. I pray they find his killer."

"Mrs. Bentley, you might be able to help with that," said Michael, leaning forward.

"Really? How?"

"Just by remembering," said Alice. "You know that you and Chef Sacha were together in the kitchen when someone put something poisonous in Harrison's salad."

"That's right," said Mrs. Bentley. "I plated those

salads myself from the bowl Chef had prepared. The two of us set them out on the table together."

"But remember, you also came into the big room where we were all having appetizers. You brought out that beautiful arrangement for the mantle."

A light dawned in the older woman's eyes. "Oh my! I'd forgotten all about that! Yes—Sully popped in saying he had the centerpieces ready, and he helped me set them on the table. It was just as well, because the chef was about to add his secret ingredient to the dinner. He always makes me leave the kitchen when he does that. What an eccentric man!"

"So you left—which means you and Chef Sacha can't be one another's alibi for that entire period of time," said Alice.

"But I was never alone," Mrs. Bentley insisted. "Sully helped me set out the arrangements, and then you all saw me come into the living room. Then Chef Sacha said dinner was ready and we all went into the dining room." She stood. "Thank you for helping to jog my memory. I'll tell the police what I know." She looked at them earnestly. "I truly want to do anything I can to help them find out who did this to our Harrison." She gave them all a sad smile and let herself out.

"The kitchen's closed for the night," said Alice. "Might be a good time to go have a peek."

"I'm feeling a bit peckish," said Owen. "Let's get dressed and go see if we can rustle up a midnight snack."

CHAPTER 12

There was a sharp chill in the air as Alice, Owen, Michael, and Franny crept through the darkness down the stone walkway to the main building.

"I think we're in for our first frost tonight," said Michael. "Which can complicate the situation with the roads even more."

"Nothing like frozen mud," said Owen. He opened the door to the main building. The room with the fireplace was cozy and warm, with only a few lamps lit and the embers still glowing in the grate. The group of friends crept through the room, then into the darkened dining hall.

"So. We're searching for secret ingredients—the deadly kind," whispered Franny as they all stole into the dark kitchen, flipping on cell phone flashlights.

"For that matter, I wouldn't mind discovering Chef Sacha's actual secret ingredient, the one he guards so carefully," said Owen, opening a cabinet and peering inside. "Whatever it is, it adds such a complex richness to his dishes."

"I even tasted it in that pasta we had at dinner," said Franny.

Alice paused and turned to Owen. "Do you have a secret ingredient in your baking?"

"Three," said Owen. "Butter. More butter. And almond extract."

"Huh. I never knew." Alice chuckled and opened a drawer, found that it was full of cooking utensils, and closed it gently. She moved over to the refrigerator. "It's unlikely the nightshade would still be here," she said, looking through its contents. "Surely Chef Sacha would be smart enough to get rid of it." She moved aside the neatly organized rows of jars on the bottom shelf. "Ooh. There's something way in the back." She bent and reached all the way to the back of the refrigerator and brought out a large glass jar. "Airtight seal," she said, flipping the metal lever to open it. "Whoa!" The aroma of the contents almost knocked her backward. She quickly closed the jar and held her flashlight to it. "What *are* these things?" Inside the jar were several small bundles, each wrapped individually in tissue paper.

"Let's have a look," said Owen, taking the jar. "Hm. No idea. Let's have a smell." He flipped the lever and the jar popped open, releasing the pungent fragrance. "That's it! That's Chef's secret ingredient! Whew!" He set the jar onto the counter. "It's stinky. But in a good way." He carefully removed one of the bundles from the jar and unwrapped it.

"Gross," said Franny, shining her light. "Looks like some kind of . . ."

"Fungus," said Michael, taking a step forward.

"I was going to say weird rotting potato," said Franny, holding her nose.

"No—I mean, it is a fungus," said Michael. "That's a white truffle!"

"Of course!" said Owen. "The chef's secret ingredient is truffles! Wow—I wonder what this jarful is worth."

"A lot," said Michael, who was already searching for information on his cell phone. "Here. According to this article, black truffles can run between three and eight hundred dollars a pound, and white truffles can cost as much as four *thousand* dollars a pound!"

Owen carefully rewrapped the truffle and placed it back in the jar. "So smelly, and yet so valuable."

"And delicious," added Michael.

"Put them back, Alice," said Owen, handing her the jar. "It makes me nervous even to hold them."

"Where do you buy truffles?" asked Alice, sliding the jar to the back of the fridge and moving the other items back exactly the way she'd found them.

"Mostly in Europe," said Michael, holding up his phone with the truffle article still open. "They're very rare and very difficult to cultivate."

"Which is why they're so valuable," said Alice.

"It says here that pigs and some dogs—"

"Okay, okay," Franny interrupted. "Truffles are fascinating and wonderful, and we can talk about them when we get back to the cottage. But they're not poisonous. Focus, people!"

"Right." Alice opened the vegetable drawer in the fridge. "How did Ben describe the poisonous plant—the nightshade?"

"Dark green leaves. Dark purple berries," said Franny.

Alice inhaled sharply. "Like this?" She pulled a plastic bag filled with dark green leaves out of the produce drawer. There were even a few berries mixed in amongst the greens. "It was buried underneath everything else."

"Oh my gosh! That could be it!" said Owen. He froze. "Did you hear that?"

"Someone's coming!" said Franny. She grabbed the bag of greens from Alice's hand, stuffed it into Owen's jacket, and closed the produce drawer, shifting Alice out of the way in the process. "Quick! To the dining room!"

They all hurried into the dining room, where a plate of cookies and a bowl of fruit had been left out on the buffet. They had all just grabbed a snack when a yawning Chef Sacha came in.

His eyebrows rose when he saw them. "Oh. I didn't realize anyone was in here."

"Just grabbing a little something," said Alice, holding up a chocolate chip cookie.

"We couldn't sleep, and Michael here gets grumpy when his blood sugar gets too low," Owen explained.

Chef Sacha nodded, wished them a good night, and crossed into the kitchen.

As they hurried back outside, Owen whispered, "And that, my friends, was suspect number one."

CHAPTER 13

"I can't believe we're doing this. I'm spooked. Can't we just go back to the cottage?" whispered Franny as they made their way back through the chestnut trees that stood just past the old chapel.

"I'm sure I saw a light moving around over here," Alice answered. "We'll just make a quick check."

"Good, because I have a bag of poisonous greens stuffed into my coat," said Owen. "It's uncomfortable."

"There's no one here," whispered Michael. "Whoever—or whatever—was holding that light is gone." He turned on his flashlight and shone it around. "See? All clear."

"Hold it," said Alice, grabbing Michael's hand

and redirecting the shaft of light. "What's that on the ground?"

"I don't see anything," said Franny.

"Someone's been digging—very recently, too, because those marks are fresh," said Alice. "Look. The ground around the bases of several of these trees has been disturbed."

"You're right," said Owen, kneeling down next to one of the chestnut trees. "The dirt is all rumpled—ooh! I see rake marks!"

"Well, that's no big deal," said Franny. "So, someone has been raking the soil. Probably Sully, whose job it is to take care of this land."

"Why would Sully come out here in the middle of the night to do the raking?" asked Owen.

"We don't know that it was Sully," Michael pointed out, squatting next to Owen and running his hands over the soil. "Still muddy, but clearly, these marks are fresh—if not, the rain would've washed them away. Hey. What's this?" He pulled a muddy nugget out of the ground.

"A rock?" asked Owen, leaning in for a closer look.

"No. It's not hard like a rock." Michael rubbed the dirt away from the item while Owen held the light on it.

"Looks just like—no way!" said Franny. "It looks like a rotting potato!"

"Smell it!" said Alice.

"I can smell it from here!" said Franny.

"I know that stink!" said Owen. "It's a truffle!" He gasped. "Oh. My. Gosh. Is *this* the monks' treasure, do you think?"

"Well, the article did say it takes ages to cultivate truffles," said Michael. "And the monks were here back in the 1800s. If they'd successfully gotten a crop going, and it somehow survived undisturbed for so many years, by now it would be—well, immense."

"But don't truffles grow in Europe?" asked Alice.

"There are a few spots in the United States," said Michael. He reopened the article on his phone and scanned it. "You have to have the right weather and soil conditions, and it does say they're usually found at the bases of particular varieties of trees."

"Like chestnut?" asked Owen.

"Yep, that is one of them," said Michael.

"Search truffles in Tennessee," said Franny.

Everyone waited while Michael ran the search. "Oh wow. There *are* truffles in Tennessee!" he said. "Very rare, but it is possible! And another thing. Truffles are generally harvested this time of year, before the first frost!"

Thunder rumbled overhead, and as if on cue, the rain began to fall.

Alice's phone vibrated. "It's a text from Luke. He and Ben are back at the cottage and wondering where we are."

"Let's go," said Owen. "We have a lot to tell them!"

"So you innocently went out to get a midnight snack and ended up finding this"—Ben held up the bag of salad greens— "and this"—he held up the dirt-covered truffle.

Doc, Zeb, and Rudy were seated in the little living room of Alice and Luke's cottage and Luke had built a fire in the woodstove. Luckily, Alice, Franny, Owen, and Michael had gotten inside before the sky really opened up and the rain started pounding the roof. *Un*luckily, the ambulance had started slipping the moment it had attempted to depart, so there would be three extra guests spending the night at The Abbey, not to mention Officers Dewey and Trimble, who were taking turns guarding the gate.

Doc took the bag of greens and turned them over, then opened them and took a sniff. He handed them over to Zeb. "I think I know what this is. What do you think, Zeb?"

Zeb took a leaf out, tore off a small piece, and to Alice's surprise, took a taste. "Yep. I believe this is Thai basil. And those are blueberries."

Alice deflated a little. "Well, it was dark in the kitchen, and—"

"And we were all hopped up on truffle fumes," said Owen. "So, these greens aren't poison. That doesn't mean Chef Sacha isn't the killer. If truffles are his prized ingredient, and he knows there are truffles on this land, just imagine how badly he must want this place. And we *think* he's thinking of buying it, because Alice and Michael heard him talking to Walter Babbage."

"Did you confirm your suspicions about how Harrison died?" Alice looked from Doc to Zeb.

Zeb shrugged. "We can't run a toxicology report or do an autopsy up here, of course. But we've checked into Harrison's health records and done a thorough examination. If I have to guess, I'd say he died last night around nine o'clock, and I'd say he ingested poison with his dinner."

"You all said he left the table not feeling well after eating his salad," said Doc. "That indicates that the poison was in the salad, and his symptoms along with our findings do support the theory of something in the nightshade family. It would be easy to hide the leaves or the berries, which do look a lot like these"—he indicated the bag of basil— "in a salad, and no one would notice a thing."

Luke got up and stoked the fire, then sat down beside Alice. "So, Harrison died around nine. But the poison would've been administered when the salads were plated—so just before we all went into the dining hall. According to Mrs. Bentley and Chef Sacha, assuming they can be trusted, they set the salads on the dining table at six thirty. We all went in to eat around seven. So that leaves about a half hour window for the killer to come in and do the deed."

"And since no one else got sick," Ben added, "the poison was clearly only added to Harrison's salad. No one else's."

"Anyone really could've done it," said Owen. "It's not like any of us were watching the dining room entrance. And the killer could've come in from outside too. It could be Sully—he came in with those centerpieces."

Alice nodded. "Or the chef could've come out of the kitchen when Mrs. Bentley went in to set the final arrangement on the mantle in the other room. Several people went outside during that time—Cate and

Juniper for sure. They easily could've walked around on the wraparound porch to the dining room and slipped in there, then slipped back out."

"Like I said," said Owen, flopping onto the couch, "square one."

Alice's mind kept going back to the truffle they'd found outside. "We need to confirm that the chef really is the person who's interested in buying The Abbey." She looked at Ben. "Walter couldn't tell us the person's name, but I bet he could tell the police."

"It's past eleven," said Luke. "Probably too late to call."

"Are you kidding?" said Owen. "It's Friday night. This is Walter and Darlene's bingo night. They're still down at the community center. And trust me, Walter *always* has his phone on him."

Ben nodded and dialed Walter's number. He clicked the speakerphone button.

Walter picked up right away. "Hey there, Captain Maguire! What can I do you for?" he asked.

In the background, Alice heard the bingo caller announce, "B-six! That's *B-six*, everyone!"

"I've got you on speaker, Walter, and I can tell you're busy, so I'll make this quick."

"Hi Walter—it's Luke," Luke put in.

"Let me guess. The gang's all there," Walter said with a chuckle.

"N-thirty-seven!" the bingo caller announced.

"You guessed right," said Ben. "Walter, I need you to confirm something as part of our investigation into the death of Harrison Huxley."

"Of course. I'm glad to help if I can," said Walter.

"You've had someone interested in buying The Abbey property, correct?"

"Yep, that's right."

Luke leaned forward. "Is it Sacha Alard?"

Walter paused. "I suppose since this is part of your investigations, I can break the rules . . ."

"You can," Ben assured him.

Walter sighed. "Yep, that's the guy."

In the background, the bingo caller said, "O-sixty-two," and then more than one person cried, "Bingo!"

"Oh boy," said Walter, "all heck is about to break loose." He held the phone away and could be heard saying, "Now Ethel, you know there can be more than one—" He put the phone to his mouth again. "Ethel Primrose is fit to be tied, folks. Call me later if you have more questions. Gotta run."

The connection went dead.

"So, Sacha prizes truffles," said Alice. "And the truffles here make this land very valuable to him."

"But he's trying to use the so-called curse on this place to buy the land at a discounted rate," said Michael.

Alice smiled at Owen. "*Not* square one."

Luke leaned forward and rested his elbows on his knees, tenting his fingers. "The only thing we know for sure is that someone on this mountaintop killed Harrison Huxley. Signs point to Chef Sacha, but the evidence is circumstantial. We have no proof. In cases like this, the thing to do is to eliminate everyone else."

Ben nodded. "The last man standing is our killer."

CHAPTER 14

"Do we think it's safe to eat breakfast?" asked Owen as they all walked to the main building for breakfast early the next morning.

"First, we don't *know* that Chef Sacha is the killer," said Luke. "And second, if he *is* the killer, I don't see that he has a motive, at this point, to harm anyone other than Harrison. No one knows that we know about the truffles."

"And third, I'm starving," said Owen. "What is it about being on vacation that makes you hungry all the time?"

"I want to talk to Juniper," said Alice, who had just spotted the woman standing on the porch, looking out over the mountains. "I know she had motive to kill Harrison—"

"Sure she did," said Owen. "He broke her heart and kept yanking her emotional chain."

"*But*," Alice continued, "my gut tells me she's the kind of person who would never harm anyone."

"She does have a gentle vibe about her," said Franny. "But we can't assume anything."

"Of course not," said Alice. "I just want to talk to her." She turned to her brother and husband. "Can we try?"

"I suppose you're going to want to do this without Ben and I?" Luke guessed.

"Well, sitting opposite two police officers can be a bit intimidating," said Alice.

"She has a point," said Franny. "We're much easier to talk to."

"People tell us all kinds of stuff," said Owen, nodding in agreement.

Ben sighed. "Fine. But we'll be right inside. Got it?"

"I'll go with them," said Michael. "Four's a crowd."

Doc, Zeb, and Rudy, who were walking over from their own cottage, met them at the door and they, along with Michael, Ben, and Luke, went inside to sit down to breakfast. Alice, Owen, and Franny walked around to the section of the porch where Juniper was standing.

"Hi," Alice said, lightly touching her shoulder.

Juniper jumped.

"Sorry!" Alice said quickly. "I didn't mean to startle you."

"No—that's okay," Juniper assured her. "I was just . . . lost in thought."

Owen and Franny had come to lean on the deck railing on Juniper's other side, and the four of them stood quietly for a moment, admiring the view.

"It's so beautiful here," Juniper said quietly. "I can't believe Harrison won't have years to enjoy it." She turned bloodshot eyes to Alice. "Your husband is the detective, right?"

"Yes," Alice admitted.

"And yours is the police captain," Juniper said, looking at Franny.

"He is," said Franny with a nod.

"And yours"—she looked at Owen.

"Mine is a concierge. And a poet," said Owen. "Not involved in law enforcement in any way."

Juniper's shoulders sagged. "You all think I killed Harrison, right?"

"No," said Alice, shaking her head. "You loved

him too much." She paused and looked at Juniper. "Didn't you?"

Juniper's eyes widened. "How did you know that? I haven't told anyone."

"I had a hunch," said Alice, not wanting to admit she'd witnessed the kiss. "Plus, I saw the way Harrison looked at you. I could tell he felt the same."

"You think so?" Juniper sniffled and rubbed her eyes.

"Juniper, can you think about where you were Thursday night between six thirty and seven? The doctor and the coroner have examined the body and have a good idea as to what killed Harrison."

"I heard them talking about poison—something Harrison ate at dinner, right?" said Juniper.

"Yes," said Alice. "Which means the killer most likely acted during that thirty minute period."

"If you can give some details about what you were doing at that time, you can clear your name," added Franny.

A crease formed between Juniper's eyebrows. "I was with all of you in the common room, having appetizers before dinner, like I told the police."

Alice silently looked at her, giving her the chance to elaborate.

"Oh!" Juniper said, slapping the railing. "I came

out here, to this porch. I was upset because—" She stopped short of finishing her sentence.

"Go on," Owen said gently.

Juniper looked at her hands. "I was upset because I had thought that Harrison invited me here this weekend to reconcile. Yes, we used to date." She gave an apologetic look. "I didn't let on that I knew him; I know. We'd dated for a long time, and I was so mortified when he suddenly broke up with me. Then I came here and found out that he'd only included me so that I could help him with this whole curse business . . . But well, we had a moment together, that evening before dinner . . . and he kissed me." She swallowed. "But then he told me he was seeing someone else—that it was *complicated*." She rolled her eyes. "That was right before we came in here for appetizers. I tried standing around making small talk, acting like everything was fine, but just couldn't do it. So, I came out here, to watch the rain and clear my head." She paused. "That probably would've overlapped that time you mentioned, so I guess I don't have an alibi."

"Think," said Owen. "Did *anyone* see you out here?"

"Well Harrison followed me, to try to talk to me again. I told him I wasn't interested in being the other woman. We talked for a little while, and then he went in. So, I guess my one alibi can't vouch for me."

"No one else saw you? Are you sure?" asked Alice.

Juniper paused. "Well Sully went by once. He had those beautiful centerpieces. He left again a while later. I think he was carrying a plate with tinfoil covering it. But he just walked by, so even he couldn't vouch for me really." She paused. "Hold it. Cate had come out at some point too, because she walked up from around the corner," she said. "But I'm not sure how long she was out here or if she'd even be willing to admit it. She doesn't like me in case you hadn't noticed."

"We did," said Owen. "You could cut the tension between you two with a knife!"

"I don't know what her problem is with me. I think she's just a nonbeliever. Probably thinks spiritualists are nothing more than delusional nutcases."

Alice caught a movement in the side of her eye and saw that it was Cate, walking slowly toward the main building from her cottage. "Harrison was seeing someone else—you said you knew that." She nodded toward Cate and then looked back at Juniper.

Juniper gasped. "Are you serious? Cate? He was seeing *Cate*?"

Alice, Owen, and Franny all nodded.

"But she's married!"

They nodded again.

Juniper released a long sigh. "Well, that *is* complicated."

"Maybe Cate noticed the way Harrison looked at you, just like we did," said Franny. "Maybe that's the real reason she doesn't like you."

"Which isn't fair," Owen added. "It's not your fault he was carrying a torch for you."

Cate approached the building, glancing at them warily as she reached for the door.

"Wait!" Juniper said. "Do you have a minute, Ms. Whitaker?"

Cate looked from one to the other of them, considering. "I guess so." She walked over to stand with them at the railing.

Alice, Owen, and Franny stood by as Juniper asked Cate to recall seeing her on the porch during the time Harrison's food would've been poisoned.

"I know it was about that time," Juniper finished, "because I remember looking at my watch and realizing it was time to go in to dinner since we were eating at seven."

Cate sighed, then looked Juniper in the eye. "I did

see you," she finally admitted. "And before that, I *heard* you."

"Heard?" Juniper frowned.

Cate put her elbows on the railing and looked down into the valley. "I'm not proud of the fact that I eavesdropped on you," she said. "I didn't mean to, really." She paused. "Actually, that's a lie. I did mean to. I saw you leave, saw Harrison watching you, saw him follow you out here . . . So I did too. But I went out one of the doors on the other side and stood right around the corner." She looked at Juniper. "I heard your whole conversation." Her face crumpled. "You were so strong!"

"Me? Strong?"

"He tried to get you back—tried to tell you that he needed time to break up with someone else—to tie up some *loose ends*." She scoffed and pointed at herself. "In other words, me. And you turned him down flat!"

Juniper laughed and shook her head. "I was about to crumble like a house of cards. Harrison had such a way with words—"

"I know! He was like a magnet. Irresistible. I can't believe I ever got involved with him! And then he expected me to end my marriage at the drop of a hat. I wasn't sure I was ready to do that—"

"Then *you* were the strong one," said Juniper.

"I was furious at him when I heard what he said to you on the balcony," said Cate. "I decided then and there to break it off with him as soon as I could get a moment alone with him. I even went to his cottage later. I wanted to get it out of the way that night. I knocked on the door for a while, but he never answered. I decided he must be asleep." She looked at Alice. "Do you think he was still alive, and if I'd just found a way to get in, I could've saved him?"

Alice shook her head. "I doubt it. Doc and Zeb have a pretty good idea of time of death. We saw you knocking at Harrison's door. It's very likely that he was already gone by then."

Cate looked at her for a moment, then sighed. "It's all so sad."

"Don't you see what's happening here?" said Owen. "*You* can recount the conversation Juniper had with Harrison," he said, looking at Cate. Then he turned to Juniper. "And *you* were heard having that conversation by her." He pointed a thumb at Cate. "You're each other's alibi!"

"He's right," said Alice. "You were both out here during that period of time when Harrison's salad was poisoned. You're off the hook!"

"Let's go tell the police!" said Cate, taking Juniper's arm.

Juniper nodded and the two went into the building together.

Owen watched after them. "They're as different as night and day. Hard to believe the same man fell for the two of them—or that they both fell for the same man."

Alice gave him a nudge. "We've just eliminated two suspects!"

"So now we've cleared Mrs. Bentley, Juniper, and Cate," said Franny.

"Levi too," said Owen. "He wouldn't have been trying to escape the killer if it was him."

"Also, Ben told me they checked into Levi's credentials," said Franny. "He just got confirmation that Levi really is a reputable private investigator with many years of experience. And between everyone's statements, it looks like he never left the room when we were having our appetizers Thursday evening."

"Then it's either the chef or the groundskeeper," said Alice. "They're the only two people left."

"My money's still on the chef," said Owen. "But we need to compel him to confess . . ." He looked at Alice. "That, or we need Harrison to come back from the dead and tell us who killed him."

Alice looked at him. "That's it! That's exactly what we're going to do!"

CHAPTER 15

By midnight, the plan was in place. It hadn't been easy, but Ben and Luke had managed to convince the entire group—which included officers Dewey and Trimble, as well as with Doc, Zeb, and Rudy—that their presence would be required at a séance led by Juniper.

"What else have we got to do? We're all stuck up here anyway," Levi, who was in on the plan, reasoned when Chef Sacha balked at the idea.

"I don't want to contact the spirits of any monks or thieves who haunt this place!" Sully protested. "This whole idea is—is creepy."

"And probably a waste of time," said Chef.

"I for one would like to give it a try," said Mrs. Bentley.

"What have we got to lose?" Cate agreed, reaching over to pat Juniper on the back.

Alice smiled at the surprising fact that the two women seemed to be on friendly terms now. Then again, it made sense in a way. They had something important in common—for all of his faults, they had both loved Harrison, and now could grieve together rather than alone.

"Harrison invited Juniper up to this mountain because he truly believed she had a gift," said Luke. "I know it's a bit unorthodox, but who knows? Maybe the spirits can tell us something."

"And by the way, I won't be reaching out to any particular spirit," said Juniper. "I'll just be looking around to see if any are present." She gave a little shrug. "Harrison's spirit might even still be here since he just passed into the next realm. Maybe we'll hear from him, and he can tell us who killed him."

"That's what we're hoping," said Luke, scanning the group for their reactions.

Alice stifled a snicker. Luke was doing a fine job of acting like he was truly hoping to get answers via the supernatural. Alice herself had cautiously believed in such things ever since she'd once booked a clairvoyant—a woman by the name of Estella Constantine—for the annual Blue Valley Fall Festival. She'd learned that while the claims of those who asserted that they were in touch with the spirit world should be taken with a grain of salt, sometimes, what might seem impossible or improbable is real, nonetheless.

The séance was to take place at midnight in the dining room, where everyone could gather around the long table. A great many candles were lit with the help of Mrs. Bentley, who was a hundred percent on board with the idea of touching base with "the other side," but had no idea that the whole thing was to be staged. Alice felt a little guilty, knowing the woman was hoping to hear from her nephew.

Owen, who would beg off saying he had a migraine, would actually be crouching just behind the kitchen door, whispering into his phone, pretending to be the disembodied voice of Harrison. His voice would come through Alice's phone, which would be set to speakerphone and tucked in her lap under the table where no one could see. Juniper, who still held out hope that they would hear from the *actual* spirit of Harrison, was prepared to let Owen speak for him if she failed to make contact. She said she'd do anything if it would help to identify the killer. Owen would wait for Juniper to say, "Tell us what you've come here to say," and then he'd begin to act as though he was about to reveal the identity of the killer. If all went to plan, the killer would be spooked enough to give themselves away.

By eleven forty-five, everyone was standing around in the fireplace room, some of them drinking coffee to stay awake, some of them looking uncomfortable, others yawning every few minutes.

"It's time," Juniper announced, coming out of the dining room. She was dressed in a flowing black skirt and purple top, and her honey-colored curls were pulled up into a loose bun on top of her head.

Everyone filtered into the dining room, which was ablaze with candlelight. Alice glanced toward the kitchen door, saw that it was open a tiny crack, and thought she could make out a sliver of Owen's shadow.

Everyone took their seats around the long table.

"We must hold hands for the duration of the séance," Juniper instructed. "Whatever you do, do not break the circle. Understand?"

Just as Alice was reaching for Cate's hand, her phone dinged in her pocket.

"Be sure to silence your cell phones," said Juniper, raising a brow at Alice.

"Sorry," Alice whispered, and quickly took out her phone. She glanced at the text message that had just come in. It was from Walter. She read quickly.

Just had a definite offer on The Abbey via email, and the address is from the office up there, so I can't tell who it's from. They signed with the initials S.A. I'm assuming it's Sacha, and he finally made up his mind to try to buy the place. I'll confirm and get back to you.

Alice felt her heart pounding wildly as she flipped her phone to silent. Sacha Alard! Or perhaps Sully . . . what had Sully's last name been? She couldn't remember. Of course, she reminded herself, just because someone was asking about buying The Abbey didn't mean they'd murdered Harrison . . . On the other hand, wanting this parcel of land, if someone was desperate to get it, could be a motive for wanting to bump off the current owner.

"Now," Juniper announced, "please close your eyes and open your minds." She took in a deep breath. "Spirits, if you are here, please, make yourselves known. We are ready to listen."

There was a pause. Alice felt a sudden rush of panic. She'd just mindlessly tucked her phone into her pocket! In her excitement over Walter's text, she'd forgotten to keep it in her lap as she awaited Owen's call—which was probably coming through right now! Alice had purposely sat next to Luke so that she could cheat a little and release his hand long enough to put

Owen on speakerphone without anyone noticing. She let go now, realizing she might have blown the whole plan. She glanced at her phone screen, hoping against hope that everyone else was following the rules and had their eyes closed. Sure enough, she'd missed Owen's call! But before she could hit redial, a voice came through, loud and clear. Thank goodness they'd thought to have a Plan B, just in case anything went wrong. Owen was to call Luke if for any reason he wasn't able to reach Alice.

Alice breathed a sigh of relief, settled back into her chair, and took Luke's hand, giving it a grateful squeeze.

"I'm here," the voice said, almost in a whisper. "Welcome."

"It is we who should be welcoming you, spirit," said Juniper. "Thank you for coming. Please. Tell us what you've come here to say."

There was a rustling sound, followed by another whisper. "I am Brother Auguste, and I have long haunted this place, trying to share my message so that I can finally find peace."

Alice frowned and glanced at Luke, who was looking at her with the same frown on his face. Owen was going rogue!

Juniper paused, then said, "We are ready to listen,

Brother Auguste." She opened one eye and looked at Alice, who gave her a confused shrug.

"The secret we guarded so carefully—the treasure . . ." The voice faded in and out as it spoke, as though the reception from the spirit realm was faulty. "I have learned that it is not to be kept. It is to be shared." This was followed by silence.

"Brother?" said Juniper. "Are you still with us?"

"I am." He sounded very far away now. "But it is time for me to go. I must share the secret of this land with you—the secret my brothers and I cultivated here, before there is any more violence . . . The treasure is—"

There was a sharp movement at the end of the table as a chair scraped against the floor.

"Is this some kind of trick?" It was a very angry Sully who had stood abruptly. He yanked his hands away from Juniper and Ben and got to his feet.

"Hold on!" Sacha said from across the table. "I want to hear what the secret is!" He looked at Juniper. "Can you get Brother Auguste back?"

"No, she cannot." Sully pulled a knife out from the inner pocket of his jacket and jerked Juniper to her feet, holding the blade to her neck.

Ben held up his hands. "No one needs to get hurt here, Sully."

"I'll kill her, I swear it," Sully warned, backing up, not loosening his grip on Juniper or the knife.

Officer Dewey stood and pulled out his gun.

"Sully, don't do anything foolish," Luke said.

"Then tell him to put down the gun," Sully said, pressing the knife into Juniper's skin.

She let out a little whimper.

"Officer Dewey, put down the gun," Ben ordered. "Sully, let's talk about this."

"I'm not interested in talking about anything with you," Sully spat, backing closer to the kitchen door. In one sudden movement, he released Juniper, threw open the door, and ran through it at top speed.

And tripped over Owen.

"Ouch!" yelped Owen.

"Grab him!" yelled Ben, going after Sully.

"I can't believe this!" said Sacha. "What is the treasure of the brotherhood? Now we'll never know!"

"I can tell you. We found it, out by the chapel, among the chestnut trees," said Owen, who was getting up from the floor, rubbing his back.

Meanwhile, Ben and Luke came back into the dining room, holding the struggling Sully by the arms.

"No!" Sully cried, attempting a lunge at Owen. "Don't you tell them!"

"Or what? You'll kill me too?" asked Owen.

Sully stilled a little, his face falling. "I found them. Harrison didn't even know about them!"

"Found what?" asked Sacha, coming over to stand next to Mrs. Bentley.

"I have no idea what he's talking about," said Mrs. Bentley.

"Truffles," said Alice.

"Truffles?" said Sacha, his jaw dropping. "No! You're kidding!"

Sully sagged.

"But that means—do you have any idea what this land is worth?"

"A lot," said Alice. She turned to Sully. "Which is why you were trying to buy it, wasn't it? Addison! That's your last name!"

"So what?"

"So Walter Babbage just got your email. You signed it with your initials and sent it from the office, but I'd bet anything it was you."

"Hold on." Chef Sacha, still confused, looked at Sully. "You were trying to buy this place too? *I* was trying to buy it. Or at least considering it. I hadn't decided yet, but—"

"But you didn't even know about the truffles," said Mrs. Bentley.

"No," said Sacha. "I just wanted to keep this place going. I wanted to be able to work here—I liked you and I thought I liked Sully, too. Harrison was a sharp businessman. I thought maybe we could make a go of it. But I had changed my mind because I was getting a little spooked."

"You can still work here!" said Mrs. Bentley. "I got a call from Harrison's attorney early this morning. He told me I'll inherit this place."

"But I thought you said that you and Harrison had talked about it, and he was donating it to charity in his will," said Alice.

"He promised me he would," said Mrs. Bentley, nodding. She smiled sadly. "But he didn't. He left it to me in spite of my telling him not to." She turned to Sacha and held out her hand. "Want to be my partner?"

Sacha's face lit up. "Are you kidding? I would be honored," he said, shaking her hand.

Mrs. Bentley walked over to Sully, who now wore handcuffs and was being escorted by Dewey and Trimble toward the door. She looked steadily into his eyes. "You could have been a partner too, if you hadn't been so selfish." Then the little woman surprised everyone when she drew back and kicked Sully right in the shin.

He cried out in pain.

"*That's* for killing my nephew!"

Everyone trailed out into the parking lot, where Sully was tucked into Dewey's squad car.

"Hasn't rained for a good while now," said Doc, looking at the sky, where a full moon was haloed by swaths of clouds. "I think we can get down the mountain." He looked at Rudy, who nodded in agreement. "Good," said Doc. "Because Mrs. Howard wants me home."

After the ambulance and police car had pulled out and disappeared down the driveway, carrying both a killer and his victim, everyone else went back into the fireplace room and stood around quietly for a few minutes, digesting the events of the night.

Finally, Mrs. Bentley spoke up. "Sacha and I hope that you will all stay on tonight."

"Rest well tonight, sleep late tomorrow, and I will serve you a fantastic brunch before you head home. How does that sound?" said Sacha.

Alice yawned and took Luke's hand. "Let the vacation *finally* begin."

As everyone walked back to the cottages in one large group, all of them exhausted between the late hour and the evening's happenings, Owen suddenly paused. "I meant to ask, which one of you did the monk's voice?"

Everyone looked at everyone else.

"It wasn't you?" asked Alice, feeling goosebumps pop out all over her skin.

"It wasn't me," said Owen. "Come on," he prompted. "Who played Brother Auguste at the séance? You're not going to tell me we actually just witnessed the undead voice of a monk who used to live on this mountain."

"Absolutely," said Juniper. "Brother Auguste's presence was very strong and very clear." She paused and looked around them, then smiled. "But he's free now."

CHAPTER 16

"So that's why Sully claimed he'd seen a grizzly bear in the woods," said Alice, putting the kettle on. She was making a pot of tea, happily back in her own kitchen at the lake cabin, where everyone had enjoyed a potluck dinner that Sunday night after arriving home.

"Yep," said Owen. "He didn't want us snooping around back in those trees, but he underestimated our bear knowledge."

"And he set the chapel on fire—twice," added Franny. "All the time trying to make the curse seem real."

Ben nodded. "He'd discovered those truffles years ago. He'd gone up the mountain to do some horticultural research because he wanted to study that grove of chestnut trees."

"The ones that had somehow managed to resist the blight," Alice recalled.

"Exactly," said Ben. "Ironically, that's also when he found that there was a healthy crop of deadly nightshade growing up there. Anyway, he'd been harvesting the truffles for years, and managing to scare away any potential buyers. He didn't want to spring for the place himself, he just wanted free reign to come and go as he pleased."

"But then Harrison came along and wouldn't be dissuaded," said Luke. "So Sully stepped up his game, hoping to either scare Harrison away or at least make the business fail by scaring away any potential guests. Then he'd go ahead and buy the place himself."

"He'd probably amassed a fortune after years of selling truffles," said Alice. "But it seems like someone would've known about his operation. I mean, don't buyers know where their truffles come from? And wouldn't Tennessee truffles have made the news?"

"He didn't want any publicity, of course, since he was stealing," said Luke. "And believe it or not, truffles are in such high demand that there's a black market for them—similar to the market for illegal drugs. Sully was starting to panic, though, because it was time to start harvesting this year's crop, and The Abbey was about to open."

"He must've been getting pretty desperate to get everyone out of the way," said Franny.

"Desperate enough to poison Harrison's salad," said Luke. "He claims he wasn't trying to kill Harrison—just make him very, very sick. He figured it would do the trick and everyone would leave."

"Well then, he had no idea who he was dealing with," said Franny.

"That's because we don't look like brilliant detectives," said Owen, arranging a batch of fresh cupcakes on a platter.

"Let's go outside for dessert," said Alice, bending to pull Izzy out of her bouncy swing.

The sun was just touching the mountaintops to the west as everyone found spots to sit on the deck, cupcakes and mugs of either autumn spiced tea or apple cider in hand. Alice wrapped her favorite cardigan sweater a bit tighter around herself as she snuggled Izzy and took a bite of a delectable pumpkin cupcake with luscious cream cheese frosting. It tasted like fall—warm and comfortable and cozy.

They were on the cusp of a busy season. There

would be fall cleaning to do, special events to host at the bookshop, Thanksgiving dinner to plan . . . there would be festivals and gatherings and parties, gifts to buy, cards to send . . .

But at this moment, as Alice savored the sweetness of her cupcake, there was only the sunset, her family, the smells of autumn, and lights coming on in windows all around the lake. For one moment, a peaceful stillness seemed to settle itself over the whole world. Alice could hear her little girl sigh, content to be back in her mother's arms. She looked over at Luke, who was watching them, his eyes full of love.

These were the treasures of Alice Maguire-Evans's life, and as Brother Auguste had said, treasures were not for keeping or guarding or hiding away, but for sharing. And in the sharing, they somehow became even more priceless.

Theo hopped up, his face now covered in frosting. "Let's go!" he said, waddling out onto the grass beyond the deck.

"I think that's his new favorite phrase," said Franny, laughing.

"Let's go!" Ben echoed his son, running after him, scooping him up, and flying him around the yard.

This excitement woke the pets, and the two dogs

ran after Ben and Theo, tails wagging, while Poppy watched from the deck, licking her paws.

"How about a sunset canoe ride?" said Owen, getting up and holding a hand out to Michael.

"Sounds great!" said Michael.

"I'm coming too!" said Franny, setting her mug on the deck railing.

They all trotted over to Owen and Michael's dock to untie the canoe.

"Hey Alice, let's take the peddle boat out!" Ben called from the lakeside. "We're challenging Owen, Michael, and Franny to a race!"

Alice gave him a thumbs-up and stood, handing Izzy over to Luke, who kissed her warmly as they made the exchange.

"Glad to be back to our crazy life?" he said, bouncing Izzy as he walked with Alice down to the water.

She took in a deep breath of fall air, smelling leaves and lake and woodsmoke from her chimney. She smiled up at her husband. "There's no place like home."

AUTHOR'S NOTE

I'd love to hear your thoughts on my books, the storylines, and anything else that you'd like to comment on—reader feedback is very important to me. My contact information, along with some other helpful links, is listed on the next page. If you'd like to be on my list of "folks to contact" with updates, release and sales notifications, etc.… just shoot me an email and let me know. Thanks for reading!

Also…

… if you're looking for more great reads, Summer Prescott Books publishes several popular series by outstanding Cozy Mystery authors.

CONTACT SUMMER PRESCOTT BOOKS PUBLISHING

Blog and Book Catalog: http://summerprescottbooks.com

Email: summer.prescott.cozies@gmail.com

And…be sure to check out the Summer Prescott Cozy Mysteries fan page and Summer Prescott Books Publishing Page on Facebook – let's be friends!

To sign up for our fun and exciting newsletter, which will give you opportunities to win prizes and swag, enter contests, and be the first to know about New Releases, click here: http://summerprescottbooks.com

Printed in Great Britain
by Amazon